A terminal glowed in the darkened chamber deep inside the residential area of the Pennines Bathosphere.

DIRK? The message played to an empty room. ARE YOU THERE, DIRK? YLON CALLING FROM THE REVENANT. AND BLAST. WE'D REALLY HOPED TO SAY GOODBYE TO YOU BEFORE WE LEFT. WE THOUGHT WE'D SEE YOU. . .

The line ended with an incomplete thought.

DIRK? PLEASE RESPOND, DIRK.

The text scrolled down as an official missive muscled it off the screen and the following verbiage appeared.

NOTICE TO ALL COUNCIL MEMBERS AND DSHQ EXECUTIVE PERSONNEL. AS OF TWELVE-HUNDRED HOURS MARS PROCLAIMED ITS INDEPENDENCE FROM THE EARTH PLANETARY ALLIANCE. WE MUST NOW CONSIDER OURSELVES IN A STATE OF WAR, AND AN EMERGENCY SESSION OF THE COUNCIL HAS BEEN CALLED AT 17:00 HOURS TO DISCUSS EARTH'S RESPONSE TO THE MARTIAN PRO-CLAMATION.

The program Dirk had written, that logged him on to the system periodically and downloaded his messages so people would think he was still somewhere within the facility, kicked in and dumped both the Lilliputs' plaintive plea and the directive into the bin.

Also in the Point SF series:

The Year of the Phial
Joe Boyle

Virus
Molly Brown

<u>The Obernewtyn Chronicles:</u>
Obernewtyn
The Farseekers

Scatterlings
Isobelle Carmody

Skitzo
Graham Marks

Strange Invaders
Stan Nicholls

The Human Factor
Random Factor
Jessica Palmer

First Contact
Second Nature
Third Degree
Nigel Robinson

Strange Orbit
Margaret Simpson

Siren Song
Sue Welford

FINAL FACTOR

Jessica Palmer

■SCHOLASTIC

Scholastic Children's Books,
Commonwealth House, 1–19 New Oxford Street,
London WC1A 1NU, UK
a division of Scholastic Ltd
London ~ New York ~ Toronto ~ Sydney ~ Auckland

Published in the UK by Scholastic Ltd, 1997

Copyright © Jessica Palmer, 1997

ISBN 0 590 19539 5

Typeset by DP Photosetting, Aylesbury, Bucks.
Printed and bound in Great Britain by
Caledonian International Book Manufacturing Ltd, Glasgow

10 9 8 7 6 5 4 3 2 1

For my sister, Alysha, last in chronological order
but not least.

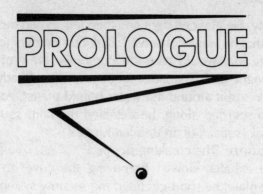

PROLOGUE

1/9/2334

Zero-hundred Hours

The party was subdued by human standards, for the warrior clones raised within the stiff confines of the military were unused to the concept of celebration. The tiny participants spoke in muted tones while Blast and Ylon, heroes of the Galactic Conflict, were particularly silent, for their human friend, Dirk Alexander, had not deigned to come to say his final farewells to his Lilliputian counterparts. Even Gwen had left early. They smiled stiffly at George Alexander and pretended to make idle chatter to cover their discomfort.

Not far from the festivities in the cargo bays that had been the clones' temporary quarters, their comrade huddled alone in the darkness of the spaceport facility. He glanced right and then left. When he was sure that he was unobserved, Dirk hurried over to the shuttle that would take the *combined* crew of the *Revenant* and *Thanatos* to their craft, already in passive orbit around the water-bound planet. As the youth scurried along, he detected the faint *squeak, squeak, squeak* of an unoiled hinge.

He froze. The creaking stopped.

He exhaled slowly. Removing the cover to the ident-plate, he short-circuited the security system by inserting a screwdriver into the complex arrangement of electronics. The shuttle door rose with a whispered *swoosh*. Again he hesitated to survey the pitch-black spaceport one last time. Then he slipped into the hold.

Not long after Dirk had vanished into the ship, a shadow stirred.

"*Squeak, squeak, squeak*," it said.

"I told you you should oil yourself," the computer system, AWS, grumbled to the servo-mech that housed it.

Robbie emitted a short, sharp whistle of querulous complaint.

"Shush," said the computer, "he'll hear us. We'll discuss this later."

The robot rolled into the shuttle, pausing only long enough to close the door behind it.

Again a hush fell upon the empty port, but only for a little while. Within the gloom, yet another shade moved. This was accompanied by a flash of bright red hair, and a young girl repeated the actions of the youthful Dirk and the servo-mech before her, removing the protective cover and shorting the mechanism. Replacing the plate, she followed the others into the once-empty shuttle.

Meanwhile, in the cargo bay, the party had reached full swing as one of the lieutenants, a little tipsy on his feet, began to sing a rousing military tune to an appreciative audience and Ylon and Blast retired to their quarters to mourn the loss of a friend.

The motion was passed and carried, and the members of the first Martian Congress of Independence looked in complete accord as they scurried to and fro, preening self-importantly. They let some clerk or underling do the menial work, drafting the proposal into a resolution and sending it to its destination.

Now was a time for posturing as the members jockeyed for the position of leadership. Gordon Rhys stood back from the rest, and he rued their decision. Almost all financial backing for major projects came from their Terran masters. OK, maybe the government didn't provide the services for Mars that they provided for everyone else, but they stayed out of the way of the locals, leaving them pretty much to their own devices. With this attitude of studied disinterest, Mars could already claim more freedom than they had on Earth or the Moon. Why this? Why now?

Oh, he'd heard all the arguments about the Lilliputian clones, but they'd never objected to newcomers in the past. In fact, they actively recruited. From what little he knew about the clones, they would be handy to have around.

Rhys grimaced. He'd always held with the philosophy "If it's not broke don't fix it". But it was too late to make them see reason. The citizens of Mars would have to make the best of it.

Around Rhys, people whispered in clusters of fours and sixes. Names were bandied about as each put forward their respective candidates and lauded their virtues. Rhys sighed. This was going to be a long night, and his prediction proved to be correct.

As the night progressed, the illusion of unity began to wear thin. Voices were raised in argument, insults exchanged. Eventually blows were struck. Rhys was noticed, leaning casually against the wall, arms crossed.

A friend joined him. Rhys shook his head in disgust. "This does not look like a group ready for self-government."

"Do you think you could do better?" The friend threw the proposal to him as a challenge.

Rhys shrugged. By the time the seventh person had stopped in his little corner with a similar proposition, Rhys could see the handwriting on the wall and he appreciated the irony.

Nearly everyone, except himself, coveted the title

of military leader and the power it entailed. And nearly everyone had a different candidate, usually themselves or a close ally. Not Rhys. He knew it would be a thankless task from the start, with the leader serving as scapegoat if they lost and subject to reprisals even if they won, for those who preferred the old ways would not applaud victory.

No one in the room, however, was willing to concede the power of ambition to another, especially if he desired it. Rhys would get the leadership by default, as a compromise candidate, precisely because he didn't want the position.

Eleven-forty-five

The sun blazed in the heavens. The ocean was reflected and refracted into thousands of sparkling diamonds that skittered gently across the water, for the wind was mild and the sea looked friendly rather than intimidating. It was, George Alexander knew in some primal part of his being, a beautiful warm autumn day.

The Union Jack stretched and snapped in the brisk southwesterly breeze. The Pennines group of associated domes and islands had chosen it as their national symbol, commemorating the old pre-flood boundaries of the British Isles with their nationhood, and harkening back to better days before Britain had become a loosely scattered group of low-lying islands and atolls.

The Pennines Complex had brought out their best for this day, which was already being called by some "Independence Day". Pennants were strung all along the top of the structure. They dripped from every antenna and line along the top of every dome that dotted the surface. Flags and ribbons snapped and flew, adding their colour to that of sun and light as it was reflected off the mirrored domes.

Below them in the port facility, normal business operations had been suspended for a day and a market had sprung up spontaneously to sell the trinkets that the more industrious residents of the dome had made in their homes to mark the day. For free enterprise was not dead yet, although it had been curtailed considerably after the last food crisis, as price controls were reintroduced and the old military-style system of assigned posts was reinstituted.

The atmosphere was carnival, far exceeding the relieved, albeit frenetic, celebrations that had followed the resolution of the last two crises. An optimism that George Alexander had never seen before was reflected in the eager faces and the happy smiles.

Resplendent light shone off the Manta Ray class cruiser where it hovered above the water. The ship was both recipient and cause of their celebration. The vessel remained a circumspect distance above the dome and waves, awaiting the arrival of the bridge crew, the last to depart from the facility. The craft presented an awe-inspiring visage to the world. The

Revenant II, as she had been dubbed, was too large to land, or to fit inside the port terminal, so final farewells to the ship and crew, who would man the first pioneering probe beyond the boundaries of the galaxy, had been moved to the top of the facility.

George Alexander eyed the sky and smiled. For once the weather had cooperated, and he was glad that he had insisted they hold the ceremony out of doors. The date, he had argued, could be rescheduled if need be, but the psychological boost the population would receive from having the sun in their faces and the wind in their hair would be immeasurable. He had been right to insist.

The platform erected specifically for this purpose had withstood all the gales that nature had thrown at it in the intervening weeks, and today both sea and sky were clear as crystal. From their station in the stands, he and the council and selected representatives of the major island-groupings could lord over the proceedings. The idea was to keep the revellers separate from the source of the revelry, lest things get out of hand, so the participants stood a level above the general population.

A second platform held the 3D vid crews from all the news networks spanning the globe: the African Highlands, the Associated American Archipelagoes, the Ural Islands, and the Asian Federation of the Himalayas and Khingan.

The shuttle that would take the Lilliputian clones

on the first leg of what would become an epic journey had been brought up from one of the launch pads to make room for the masses below. All the remaining lift-pad doors bar one had been left open so those on "ground-level" could see. And still it was not enough. People were squeezed as tight as sardines in a tin, and still more were pouring into the terminal until they were pressed shoulder to shoulder, unable to move without concerted effort.

The brave had clambered on to the plasti-glas dome. They clung, without a secure perch, to the struts that held the plates of plasti-glas together and tried to ignore the stomach-wrenching view of the floor hundreds of metres below their feet where the "ground" seethed with human life as relentlessly as the ocean waves.

The shuttle that would take the bridge crew to the mother ship had been polished to a blinding whiteness. Before it the Lilliputs stood to attention, arrayed in full battle regalia of the now-defunct military. Ribbons hung from visor and cap while braids garnished seam and sleeve, so the warrior clones blazed as brightly as their ship. Fire glinted from its wings and the sun formed a backdrop of deepest sapphire.

Breathtaking!

George Alexander exhaled slowly. Just the shot in the arm the peoples of the Earth needed. For this rite was more than a simple farewell to the heroes of old. Mankind had pinned all hopes, prayers and wishes on this flight. Indeed the entire future of the species – both the tall and the small – hinged upon the success of this mission. If the little people prospered, so would their human forebears. Thus the voyage marked a declaration of independence from the captivity that had gripped humanity since the Flood and the Exodus kept man bound to a water-logged world and its two colonial bodies, the Moon and Mars.

Since that time, man had trodden the treadmill of servitude to the planet he had destroyed, but now he could expand his range into the stars. For the warrior clones, it would be little more than a hop, skip and a jump to get to the mother ship, but for humankind, it was a huge leap.

The band, rusty from lack of use, struck up an off-key, if robust, version of *God Save the Queen*, and George wondered how many people remembered the words any more. A token royal had been dug up from DSHQ somewhere, where he worked in accounting. He looked ill at ease, drowning under the robes and chains of office that the council members had pressed upon him.

George Alexander glanced at the Lilliputian champions of the Galactic Conflict, Ylon and Blast. The two glittered in their uniforms of tinsel and gold braid while their faces were masks, expressing neither joy nor pride at the honour done them.

Mr Alexander's gaze shifted from Ylon and Blast to

the empty chair beside his own which should have been occupied by the only human hero of the war, his son Dirk.

Poor form, George thought, that the lad should refuse to attend the ceremony – worse even than missing the party last night. Alexander frowned. He knew Dirk was angry and hurt that his friends should leave him behind. Like the rest of the population, he wanted to go with them, but this display of temper was childish, petty. George was going to have to have a serious talk with his son when this was over. He was missing an event of historical significance, an event that Dirk had been instrumental in creating. Someday the boy would rue the loss of the memory that so many others shared.

The Minister of Food grimaced; the only one he was really hurting was himself. Then he noticed the pinched expression on Ylon's and Blast's faces and he realized that Dirk's absence hurt them too. George shook his head.

Foolish boy!

The song ended with a minor chord, which George was sure wasn't supposed to be there. With its completion, people sat, leaned against their fellows or clung to struts as their position permitted.

The Chief Administrator cleared his throat nervously and threw George an enquiring look. His gaze flicked to the empty chair and back again. George shrugged and the band launched into another ditty.

The crowd grew restless, and Administrator Alfred Barrymore-Smythe shuffled, reflecting their unease. A quiet, unassuming little man, he did not look like the head of the government. Neither did he act the part – it had taken quite a bit of coaxing to persuade him to speak. Yet as chief administrator, Barrymore-Smythe oversaw the co-ordination of all departments, from Employment and Social Security, Business and Finance to Health, Energy, Water and Food. He was the closest thing the loosely associated council members had to a head.

The final strains of song were whisked away by the wind. The chief rubbed his hands against his thighs and sauntered toward the podium. The crowd cheered.

Barrymore-Smythe leaned forward, pressed his lips to the microphone, and reverb screamed throughout the speaker system. He blenched, and it fell silent.

George pursed his lips. Some things, it seemed, never changed. The administrator advanced more cautiously toward the mic.

"Test. Test. One. Two. Three. Test."

"We hear ya, Fred."

The chief administrator blushed and the crowd roared with laughter. He grinned.

"My friends, we are gathered here today not only to say goodbye to dear friends ..."

A snarl echoed through the assembly.

"... who must be thanked for their heroics in the last crisis and their generosity in the first..."

A heckler shouted, "I'll say, after nearly blowing us away!"

Barrymore-Smythe hurried on as if no one had interrupted. "We wish them well on this their final quest, the deep space probe to the stars..."

The Lilliputian clones stepped forward, clicked their heels, bowed and entered the shuttle.

The Captain Zona Gametal Zed was greeted by his yeoman as soon as he entered the ship. They hastened to the bridge as she gave her report.

"The passengers have settled nicely. They are strapped in and ready to go."

Zed inclined his head, acknowledging the *Revenant*'s other, unspoken "mission": to transport their peers to their new land base on Mars. If it became common knowledge that the clones had received lucrative land grants often denied their human counterparts, it would raise a hue and cry that could reverberate around the world. But with the Earth's resources already stretched to the limit, any decrease in the number of mouths to feed was a welcome relief and if the clones were removed from the parent, Earth-bound population, who resented their Lilliputian offspring, so much the better.

Those who had elected for Martian resettlement

had been secreted aboard the *Revenant* last night, along with the regular crew.

The yeoman continued as they entered the bridge. "The preliminary calculations have been input into the computer."

Captain and crew fanned out across the bridge, taking their stations. Captain Zed surveyed his team. Next to Zed, his twin and one-time enemy, Captain O. Zeta Cyte, mimicked his movements.

The crew stood at ease, feet planted wide and arms tucked behind their backs, relaxed but ready to swing into action when the order was given. Few would have guessed that they faced possible extinction.

Not one of them knew what lay beyond their galaxy. Only the sketchiest information was available about the outer strip of planets, from Uranus to Pluto. For man's curiosity had been seriously dampened by the flood. The outer planets had been judged uninhabitable. Not that they were any more or less habitable than Mars or any one of the lunar satellites upon which mankind had made a home, but man was not interested in conquering a new and increasingly hostile environment until he had mastered the old ones.

The hope was that the *Revenant* would discover a habitable, or Class M, planet beyond the stars. Zed chuckled at the phrase – terminology dating back to science fiction of old, yet whether one thought of M

14

for maintenance – able to maintain the human life form – or M for man, it worked. So why change it?

While little was known about the outer rim, even less was known about Centauri. The same indifference that coloured man's perspective on the outer planets within his home galaxy had warped his view on others, and little research had been done into what was deemed an unattainable goal.

Would the crew find a habitable planet? For that matter, would they find any sort of planetoid or planetary body? Or would they be forced to travel on, from galaxy to galaxy? Would they and their offspring spend their lifetimes searching for a place to alight and rest? Would they even survive the trip? Zed snorted. The relatively untried engines might explode or implode and the hull crumple under the sustained pressure of the leaps. The ship's star drive had only been tested as far as the Chiron rim, and for that reason, the three shift captains had agreed to take the voyage in a series of jumps. The trip would take longer that way, but they would be relatively assured of their arrival. Each leap would be of longer duration than the one before, thus they would test the endurance of the engines as they went.

The captains reckoned, if things went well, an ETA of less than a year in real time, although how long it might be in subjective time, they could only guess.

Zed scanned their expectant faces again. Not a

single expression betrayed either doubt or trepidation.

He nodded to the engineer, or chief technical officer, Xi.

"All right, calculate wind velocity and vector versus the distance to the facility."

There wouldn't be an actual take-off, since the Manta-style cruiser did not need a launch pad to provide impetus; but the council wanted to give the public one last show to awe and inspire them. So, rather than trundling off into space, the *Revenant II* would perform a timed-leap, vanishing into ultra-space while still within visual sighting of the bathosphere.

Because of their proximity to the facility, extra care had to be taken to avoid swamping the people on top of the dome. The blast of the implosion from the resulting displacement of air might cause a hurricane, if they weren't careful, or a tidal wave.

"Aye, aye, sir," said Xi.

"Take us to the lunar side of the planet just beyond Earth's atmospheric mantle, where we will await the go-ahead for the leap to Mars from DSHQ."

The ship disappeared with a boom like a thunderclap, and the crowd went wild. Caps flew, arms were flung towards the heavens – inadvertently clipping many an ear – or around the nearest neck as humanity cheered. And cheered. And cheered. An affirmation of themselves.

Until they'd screamed themselves hoarse.

Meanwhile, in the deserted Deep Space HQ, AWS chattered to life. Its comforting mechanization was lost on a nonexistent audience. Then the laser on the remote communication network flashed and the printer spat out a single page of text as the following words appeared on the screen:

URGENT: PRIORITY ONE

DATE: 1/9/2334

TIME: 12:00 GMT TERRAN STANDARD

FROM: THE FREE REPUBLICS OF MARS

TO: THE CONFEDERATED ARCHIPELAGOES OF EARTH

SUBJECT: DECLARATION OF INDEPENDENCE

WE, THE CONSOLIDATED PEOPLE OF MARS, DIEMOS AND PHOBOS HAVE CHOSEN BY COMMON CONSENT TO SECEDE FROM THE COLONIAL PLANETARY ALLIANCE. IN ADDITION WE DO DENY EARTH'S RIGHT TO GRANT LAND UPON THE COMBINED LAND MASSES OF MARS, DIEMOS AND PHOBOS.

WHEREAS SUCH LAND WAS DEEDED TO THE INHABITANTS IN PERPETUITY;

WHEREAS SAID DEED SPECIFICALLY GRANTED THE INHABITANTS THE RIGHT TO SELF-RULE, IN ESSENCE GRANTING THEM SOVEREIGNTY;

WHEREAS SAID INHABITANTS WERE GIVEN THE RIGHT TO EXPAND AS POPULATION REQUIRED;

WHEREAS THE LAND GRANTED, 0 DEGREES LATITUDE AND 110

LONGITUDE, OTHERWISE KNOWN AS THE THARSIS MONTES, INCLUDES ONE OF THE MORE HABITABLE PORTIONS OF THE PLANET. SAID LAND HAS ALREADY BEEN CLAIMED AT GREAT RISK TO LIFE AND LIMB BY THE RESIDENTS OF THIS PLANET.

WHEREAS TO RELINQUISH SAID HABITABLE LAND WOULD REQUIRE EVACUATION OF THE RESIDENTS, INCURRING HARDSHIP AND LEAVING THEM HOMELESS.

WHEREAS THE DULY APPOINTED BODY HAS DEEMED THE LIL-LIPUTIAN CLONES TO BE CITIZENS OF EARTH. AS CITIZENS, SAID WARRIOR CLONES WILL BE SUBJECT TO ALL THE LAWS OF IMMIGRATION AS SET FORTH BY THIS BODY.

IN ADDITION WE, THE UNITED PEOPLE OF MARS, ISSUE THIS FORMAL DECLARATION OF INDEPENDENCE EFFECTIVE AS OF TWELVE-HUNDRED HOURS (GMT EARTH-STANDARD) THIS DAY. THE MARTIAN PEOPLES WILL HENCEFORWARD BE KNOWN AS THE FREE REPUBLICS OF MARS.

UNTIL WE RECEIVE OFFICIAL RECOGNITION OF THIS, OUR LEGITIMATE CLAIM, FROM EARTH, WE WILL REMAIN IN A STATE OF READINESS FOR WAR, AND ANY ACT BY EARTH OR HER LUNAR COLONIES TO INTERFERE WITH THE DUE PROCESS OF LAWFUL SEPARATION WILL BE CONSIDERED AN ACT OF AGGRESSION OF ONE SOVEREIGN WORLD UPON ANOTHER AND MEET WITH VIOLENT REP-RISAL BY THE MARTIAN AUTHORITIES.

Meanwhile another more discreet communique was circulated among all the ports and outposts along the loose network of communities that was Mars.

URGENT: PRIORITY ONE CALL.

AS OF TWELVE-HUNDRED HOURS GMT (EARTH STANDARD), THE

COMBINED PEOPLES OF DIEMOS, PHOBOS AND MARS HAVE ISSUED A DECLARATION OF INDEPENDENCE FROM THEIR TERRAN MASTERS.

FOR ALL PRACTICAL PURPOSES, WE ARE AT WAR. PORT AUTHORITIES ARE ORDERED TO IMPOUND ALL SHIPS FOR USE IN THE FREE REPUBLICAN ARMY, NAVY AND AIR CORPS. ALL VEHICLES CARRYING EARTH'S FLAG ARE TO BE DETAINED WHILE INCOMING VEHICLES ARE TO BE CONFISCATED AND ALL THEIR CARGOES SEIZED.

Then, using the vast structure of the system against itself, the provisional government entered the mastermind computer, AWS, freezing all Earth-linked assets on Mars.

1/9/2334

Fourteen-hundred Hours

Footsteps echoed down the narrow maintenance corridor.

"It's him."

Dirk lifted his leg and halted, foot still aloft. He listened carefully, his body canted slightly forward.

"Squeak."

His face, already pale, bleached even more until it was little more than a white smear weirdly lit by the tentative illumination given off by the radiant floorboards.

"Who's there?" he said.

Silence.

He replaced his foot on the floor and continued walking.

Not good. Less than two hours aboard ship and he

was hearing voices when logic and reason told him that he should be safe – for a little while, at least.

The final shuttle, with captains and bridge personnel, had docked, and all hands were summoned to greet their leaders for this the "virgin voyage" of their ship. This misnomer was something of a euphemism, for the *Revenant II* had been through rigorous testing and retesting of each and every function, system and subsystem. The craft had made several jumps to Mars and to the Chiron rim and back again.

The months of checks had given Dirk time to find a lair, and he'd picked his location well, in a dead-end elbow curve in the endless piping and conduits that snaked along the dark underbelly of the ship. His berth was ideally situated directly below the living quarters, equidistant from the kitchens and the sanitation facilities.

The youth turned the final corner with a quick glance over his shoulder and ducked into his hideaway. He examined the place that would be his home. The L-shaped room was perfect for his needs, allowing him to store his gear in one part of the bend and set up housekeeping in the other. A green light burned steadily in the background, indicating that the machine buried in the back wall was functioning with optimum efficiency – another reason why he'd chosen this room. He would have warning of imminent invasion if the mechanism ceased to work properly.

Even if the equipment did break down, the odds were that the crew would send a maintenance droid to effect repairs, and droids exhibited no inquisitiveness whatsoever about anything beyond their assigned task. Of course the Lilliputs might send a droid with a remote camera, but Dirk had hedged his bets, having ordered and supervised the inspection of this particular piece of machinery and had studied it himself. If the light switched from functional green to probationary yellow, he could repair it.

Dirk stretched and yawned, his fingers barely grazing the ceiling. In a ship originally built for big people, there was more than enough room for him to stand fully upright. He sauntered across the tiny cubicle, furnished with a collapsible table, a folding chair and a bedroll that he could push out of the way during the day.

He flopped into the chair and reviewed the steps that had brought him to this pass. He couldn't put his finger on a single thing that had triggered his final rebellious act.

The idea of leaving on the Manta-class vessel had occurred to Dirk the first time he clapped eyes on her. She was a beauty; she was built for speed, and she was built for those of human stature. He'd always wanted to explore the stars. Suddenly the dream became achievable – until Finn presented the ship to the Lilliputian clones.

Then disillusionment set in as Dirk recollected people's reaction to him during the crisis. All this power as head of DSHQ, and yet no one had heeded him or believed him about the Manta until the Lilliputs had arrived on the ship. Then man had reacted true to kind – violently and with little forethought as to what the consequences of his actions might be. Meanwhile, in an attempt to regain war-time stability, government ministers re-implemented many of the old war programs – a step back into the past.

Dirk was forced back into the schoolchair that registered a student's presence with retinal scans and palm-print examination and ratted on him if he absconded. Treated just like any kid, supposedly to set a good example, and not even AWS could be persuaded to disable the system.

Nowhere was this reversion to type more poignantly represented than by his relationship with his father. The man had become simply impossible. His father was always nagging at Dirk, demanding more of him, and now they fought constantly.

Once all the subsystems were back on line, tedium replaced disillusionment and Dirk, pinned to his schoolchair, grew bored. When he made his first preliminary examinations, it was just a game – something to keep him occupied.

He had the computer calculate the amount of food

he'd need to meet minimal nutritional requirements. Then he researched the availability – how much food was in the Lilliputian stores versus how much he might feasibly consume before it was noticed.

He did the same thing for space. He ran probability studies on detection – one hundred per cent when he considered his size versus that of the clone. Lastly he played with the odds, studying the layout of the ship, picking locations and checking the percentage risk of discovery.

Once the idea had occurred to him, it fascinated him. He found himself developing different stratagems. Could he store food, thereby eliminating detection due to lost stores?

Of course the statistics changed, depending upon the amount of time spent in transit, and here Dirk could use his position as Director of DSHQ to improve the odds, experimenting with routes until he could manipulate them to his best advantage.

Eventually the odds had improved to almost zero, and still he toyed with the idea, unwilling to set it aside. There were logistical hurdles to be overcome, and he found himself checking the reserve of dried foods, or "camp food", that had become so popular after the last crisis, and placing an order, just as a joke. Aboard ship, he used his time during testing and flights to explore every nook and cranny with his friends Ylon and Blast until he knew the ship like the back of his hand. Still he dallied, unable to make up his mind.

It had been Gwen's rejection that had pushed him over the edge. To this day, he didn't even know why – what had happened or what he had done wrong. He ran his fingers through his black hair and winced. Apart from Gwen, the Lilliputian clones Ylon and Blast – and the computer system AWS – were the only friends Dirk had. And Ylon and Blast were leaving.

Suddenly, what had begun as a game, a simple mental exercise, became urgent. It became real as he opted to follow his friends. Who else did he have?

He could scratch Gwen. He'd miss AWS, but it was only a computer, and if he needed to, or wanted to, he could always link up with the system via the ship's mainframe.

He lifted a single shoulder in a shrug. Gwen's rebuff didn't matter now. He had severed his ties with her, as he had severed his ties with his family and Earth ... for ever.

He pushed the finality of the thought away. Others would follow him into space eventually. They must.

It had been difficult enough sneaking on board. His height was a dead giveaway. He had had to stow away the night before, so that he could slip on to the *Revenant* during the chaos that ensued while the clones were smuggling their passengers aboard the craft. Even then he'd had to wait until everyone had disembarked and the shuttle refuelled. The crew was whizzing through the preflight checklist on their way to pick up the next load of passengers, as he slunk from the shuttlecraft and into the cargo bay. He'd barely made it.

Dirk shifted uncomfortably in his chair. He could have sworn he'd seen another shadow sliding away from the ship out of the corner of his eye as he entered the ventilation duct. Later he thought he heard the *squeak, squeak, squeak* of a wheel that needed oiling somewhere up ahead of him, although he reasoned it was probably a maintenance droid. He'd withdrawn into a side bore for a long time, until the robot had the time to get wherever it was going. No use tempting fate.

Since that time, Dirk couldn't shake the feeling of being watched. He shivered. Then he stood up, paced to the back of the L and peered into the storage area.

He saw nothing amiss, only the collection of assorted oddments and boxes he thought he might need in his new life.

The youth spun round and, feeling before him with his toe, edged his way back to tip of the L where it joined the maintenance corridor and stared down the hall.

Empty.

The crew would be busy preparing for launch, and at this late date, there should be little to repair and no reason to frequent this portion of the ship. Or there'd better not be. Dirk harkened back to the squeaking droid. It didn't bode well that a valuable piece of equipment should be malfunctioning so early in the voyage – before the journey had even begun.

Errors, at this time, could be fatal. Dirk wiped his brow as if he could wipe away his doubts with the back of his hand.

Just then the propulsion engines began to rev. His ears pricked, his head tilted to one side. They should have switched to star drive. The *Revenant* was supposed to jump this first leg of the voyage to Mars.

Something must've gone horribly wrong.

AWS noted the scuffle-thud of Dirk's footsteps through its microphone input as they retreated down the hall. The boy would have to learn about silence if he wanted to remain undetected. The computer did a heat scan of the area and detected no life-forms besides Dirk.

The sound of the youth's strides dwindled, and electricity surged through AWS's circuits, not unlike a human releasing adrenaline into the bloodstream.

Robbie gave a long, low whistle.

"I told you coming here was a bad idea," AWS griped. "I mean, it's all very noble to want to check up on your charge and make sure he's OK – as if anything *could* happen to Dirk here – but the probabilities of a 60-cm by 45-cm box being discovered in a two-cubic-metre space in the next twenty-four hours are nine-thous—"

An exasperated squeal overrode the number.

"All right, so you don't care about statistics, but you do care about discovery, don't you? You don't want to be sent back while Dirk goes on to Alpha Centauri, do you?"

Robbie chirped.

"Well, if we don't exit before he returns, we're stuck with odds of—"

The boxy body of Robbie bounced up and down in agitation, eliciting a noise like a raspberry from its air-cushioned shock absorbers.

"I wish you'd stop that. It's – " AWS faltered as the computer searched for the right word – "rattling."

AWS reviewed the plans of the ship.

"There's a 45-by-75-cm niche that has the required B352 serial port approximately 20 metres to your right. Will that be close enough for you soothe your uneasiness about your ward? You can check on Dirk as often as you like, you worry wart," AWS grumbled.

Robbie gurgled his assent and rose majestically like a square sun above the rest of the boxes. The servo-mech rolled over them, bumping into the chair as it moved into the long part of the L.

"Will you watch where you're going? You are not limited to human visual range, you know," muttered AWS. "Wait a second."

Robbie squeaked to a halt.

"We've got to fix that wheel." AWS surveyed the immediate environment, using his infrared and X-ray enhanced sensors that had been embedded in Robbie's photoreceptor. This not only enabled the computer to trace the electric wiring and fibre optics "visually", as pulses of current, *through* the metal exoskeleton of the wall, but also revealed any warm-blooded creatures larger than, say, your average gnat.

"It's OK."

The newly combined AWS-Robbie creaked down the access ramp to the corridor.

AWS continued to gripe. "Honestly, you're as bad as any nanny."

Robbie used its voice box for the first time. "It is in my programming to attend to charges, especially the little ones."

"I'm fully cognizant of the specs for the F-19007 Servo Mech, Family Service model," AWS informed Robbie. "Dirk is not so little, if you ask me."

The robot warbled an enquiry.

"Yes, I know we have covered 20 metres, but I was giving a straight-line, as-the-crow-flies distance. As if there were no bulkheads or corridors. There are."

The servo-mech prepared to object with a great out-rushing of air, but AWS forestalled the other's protests. "It is the closest place with all the necessary requirements, the appropriate hook-up and just the right size. We shall fit quite nicely. Once in place, we'll blend in and become part of the wall. Just don't talk to anybody. Remember, your model isn't supposed to have the capacity. The presence of a voder in a F-19007 Servo Mech, Family Service model might arouse suspicion.

"In fact, I recommend that the best way to avoid detection is to shut down. That", AWS concluded with an air of resolution, "is what I intend to do."

The computer system imitated a human yawn. "Just loitering about until we get somewhere would be boring, and a bit of a nap would be nice."

AWS added almost as an afterthought, "Turn left here and proceed about 10 metres."

Squeak, squeak, squeak, Robbie replied as he measured out the distance.

"Remind me to oil you," said AWS. "Ah, here we are. Another left. Proceed three metres, and voilà! Home."

The robot eyed the aperture with a rolling of photo-receptor cells.

"You'll fit. Trust me."

Robbie spluttered, spun around one hundred and eighty degrees and backed into the hole. The wall became seamless. Only if they were looking for it would repair crews miss the inlet and power sources that the niche contained. The effect, however, was more than slightly marred by the apron the servo mech insisted on wearing.

"I wish you'd take that ridiculous thing off," said AWS. "You look like you're wearing curtains."

Robbie maintained a stoic silence. AWS listened for a bit, assumed the robot had taken its advice and powered down. AWS sighed. Inside the box-like body that now held a cloned copy of the master system AWS the following words flashed on the mini VDU ...

THIS IS AWS SIGNING OFF

The screen went dark and Robbie was left alone with its own thoughts.

Ylon scowled at the communications console. Blast hovered just over his shoulder.

"Any answer from Dirk?"

"No, but he's wiped the last message so that must mean he's received it. Just to be on the safe side, I'll leave another one."

Blast leaned against the console, arms crossed, and chewed on her lip. She averted her gaze from her partner. Neither one wanted to give vent to their feelings. It was pretty shabby treatment after their months of friendship.

Perhaps, as some of their counterparts claimed, all big people were alike and couldn't be trusted. Either way, she couldn't get shut of this place quickly enough. She was tired of Terra and she was tired of having big people look down on her.

Snatches of conversations came to Blast as their

fellow crew members performed the routine pre-jump checks before their departure to Mars.

Captain Gametal Zed repeated the procedure step by step. "Computers?" he barked.

Replies came to him from various areas of the bridge and beyond.

"Ultra-space program on-line," said the systems analyst from his console.

"Capacitors?"

A voice floated through the intercom from the far engineering decks. "Check."

"Conductor coils?"

"Fully functional."

"Electrical output?"

"100 per cent of optimum," said Chief Technical Officer Xi.

"Conversion?"

"Operational."

"Engine function?"

"Raring to go." Xi grinned and winked at his commander. "This baby's ready, Captain."

"All right, calculate the jump."

"Done, Captain," said Xi.

"Recalculate."

"Aye, aye, sir." He snapped into a salute before keying in the coordinates.

This leap would be a much easier jump than the first one. There was a minor probability that they might materialize inside a solid object – if they miscalculated the position of the planet and its moons, either by orbit or the seasonal declination; but Mars's path had been plotted centuries ago by the ancients, and only a collision of cataclysmic proportions with a major asteroid like Eros, Icarus, Apollo or Hidalgo could deflect it from its course.

Still, it was always better to be safe than sorry.

Finally Zed's gaze lit up the communications officers, Ylon and Blast.

She shook off her mood. This was no time for sorrow or regrets. They were about to take off on one of the greatest adventures mankind had ever known.

Blast levered herself away from the console, bowed slightly to her commander and hurried to her seat.

"Any word?" said Zed.

"Not yet, sir," answered Ylon.

"I wonder what's keeping them." The captain glanced at the chronometer display; two hours had passed – more than enough time for the council to make it back to DSHQ, no matter how congested the port-dome was.

"The route still checks out, A-OK, Captain," Xi announced.

"Very goo—"

But Zed's statement was drowned out as Blast gasped out loud.

Zed lifted a single brow in enquiry. "Yes, Lieutenant?"

"A message has arrived, sir."

"Good. Prepare for—"

Blast interrupted. "It's not the one we were expecting, sir."

"What do you mean?" Zed said.

"Mars has declared war on Earth."

"What!" His voice rose a notch.

"It would appear, sir, that Mars has declared its independence from the Terran Alliance, and we are now at war. We've been ordered to proceed to Mars at normal propulsion speeds while they follow diplomatic channels to try and negotiate a peace."

Strength drained from his legs, and Zed sagged into his seat.

A terminal glowed in the darkened chamber deep inside the residential area of the Pennines Bathosphere.

DIRK? The message played to an empty room. ARE YOU THERE, DIRK? YLON CALLING FROM THE REVENANT. AND BLAST. WE'D REALLY HOPED TO SAY GOODBYE TO YOU BEFORE WE LEFT. WE THOUGHT WE'D SEE YOU . . .

The line ended with an incomplete thought.

DIRK? PLEASE RESPOND, DIRK.

The text scrolled down as an official missive muscled it off the screen and the following verbiage appeared.

NOTICE TO ALL COUNCIL MEMBERS AND DSHQ EXECUTIVE PERSONNEL. AS OF TWELVE-HUNDRED HOURS MARS PROCLAIMED

ITS INDEPENDENCE FROM THE EARTH PLANETARY ALLIANCE. WE MUST NOW CONSIDER OURSELVES IN A STATE OF WAR, AND AN EMERGENCY SESSION OF THE COUNCIL HAS BEEN CALLED AT 17:00 HOURS TO DISCUSS EARTH'S RESPONSE TO THE MARTIAN PROCLAMATION.

The program Dirk had written, that logged him on to the system periodically and downloaded his messages so people would think he was still somewhere within the facility, kicked in and dumped both the Lilliputs' plaintive plea and the directive into the bin.

1/9/2334

Fourteen-thirty

Twelve very disturbed and disgruntled individuals gathered in the boardroom at DSHQ for this unexpected meeting. Once they'd scattered to home or work after the hour-long ceremony, it had taken a while before word had filtered to each of them and they were able to reconvene. Dirk Alexander, as director of Deep Space HQ, should have been the unlucky thirteenth. George Alexander eyed the clock as four minutes past the hour slid into five. The boy was late.

George scowled. This was a meeting of national – nay, international – importance, in which their government would have its say. Although the voice of the elected ministers of this sovereign land would be just one among many, according to the by-laws of the new constitution of global confederation that had replaced the military, so it was similar in structure to the old European union.

Well, if Dirk wouldn't condescend to attend...

Some of the ministers were caught in animated conversation while others, aware of all the potential ramifications, remained silent.

"I would've expected it from the Moon – they're always causing trouble – but Mars!"

The loss of Mars from the alliance was of no great importance. A mining colony, producing everything from minerals to hoarfrost, it provided few goods that Earth, with its lack of an industrial base, could use.

Yet if the Martians got away with it, it wouldn't be long before the Lunar colony followed suit.

Prices would sky-rocket, and a food crisis ensue that would make the last seem mild. Earth would starve. For the Moon had advantages that Terra had not. It could and did recycle water, in all its many forms. As the Earth's population expanded more domes were built, all needing internal water supplies. But as Mars became more established and refined its technology, its production of ice would increase and Lunar need for Earth's only resource would dwindle.

The Alliance ensured that the Terran population ate. The Alliance must be preserved at all costs, even if Mars was superfluous to Earth's needs.

In interplanetary relations Mars had always been treated like the poor cousin. The planet's allegiance to Earth was nebulous at best. The Lunar colony had been planned and constructed by Earth during the Exodus, but the Martian colonists had gouged their settlements from the Martian soil without assistance. The first immigrants were those rejects who could not survive within the insular society of the Lunar domes and had escaped to the nearest large body – the true pioneers of their period.

Barrymore-Smythe cleared his throat, interrupting George's thoughts. The chief administrator leaned over and whispered into his ear, "Where is Dirk?"

"I don't know. The summons went through on the computer and he picked it up. He should be here. I can't imagine why he isn't, or where he is."

"Should I start? I mean as head of Deep Space HQ this is really his sphere, not mine."

"Well, we can't wait until the boy decides to put in an appearance."

The chief administrator frowned. "I suppose not."

He tapped his spoon against his cup. "Attention, attention, if you please, ladies and gentlemen. I call this first war council to order."

A hush descended on the group as all pondered the possibility of war without a military structure to support it.

"We have", Barrymore-Smythe said, "received this ... uh ... missive from our Martian colonies –" He threw the piece of paper on the table – "which you have all read by now. In front of you, you will find folders that contain the original land grant, or deed, under which the Martian colonies were formed. I'm sure you have all taken the time to acquaint yourselves with the message and the situation. To summarize, it would appear that we've given away a town that already exists, and they are understandably angry."

"Of course," said Raman Murti, Minister of Employment and Social Security. "Who wouldn't be?"

"Is there any truth to this claim of sovereignty?" said Frank Schwartz, energy minister.

"The grant does give them limited self-rule – the right to elect local leaders or solve territorial issues without our intervention," said Barrymore-Smythe.

"Interpreted loosely," said George, "this could be construed as falling into the latter jurisdiction. The right to grant land."

Barrymore-Smythe explained, "However, the deed does firmly state that Mars is a colony and rule reverts back to Earth should the planetary government be unable to function, and in matters of conflict, Terran law supersedes Martian law."

"What about the previous land grants?" pressed Murti. "Are definite tracts specified?"

"In fact, they are written down to the minute and degree of latitude and longitude."

"Ah ha!" said Norm Bandy, Minister of Water and

the Environment. "We got 'em then, on both points of law."

"Not exactly. There is a clause which allows them to relocate should the designated area be deemed uninhabitable."

Bandy snorted. "All Mars is uninhabitable."

"So is Earth," commented Germaine Austin, Minister of Health and Education.

"Agreed," Norm sniffed and crossed his arms. "You won't get any argument from me, which only reconfirms the fact that there should no real reason for change."

"Be that as it may," Barrymore-Smythe held a single finger up for silence, "they still have that right to move as long as they register the new location with the Bureau of Colonial Development. We used those lists to determine the coordinates, for the Lilliputian grant. You see we were trying to find a position close to another settlement, so that the Lilliputs didn't have to start out completely alone."

"Obviously, the register is incomplete."

"Obviously."

"In which case," said Norm, "they don't have a leg to stand on."

"On the contrary, the regulations do not require that the Martians register communities that have expanded beyond their original bounds. Neither do they have to register new communities made up completely of the indigenous population."

"But", argued Frank Schwartz, energy minister, "the Martians are always recruiting people, especially those with engineering and technical skills, so how can these communities be made up of natives?"

"Remember that the definition of indigenous population on a planet where everyone is a transplant must, of necessity, be vague. Who knows if this territory we have granted covers land with an offshoot community? Perhaps the nearby settlement has expanded into the assigned territory. A census taken every decade on a planet like Mars is woefully inadequate. Either way the law does not require registration, and it would appear somebody already lives there. As I said, the inhabitants are understandably upset, as we would be if someone decided to take over this facility."

"Just like the Native Americans," mumbled George, and everybody stared at the ground as they digested his comment.

"Has anybody contacted Central?" enquired Bandy, referring to the planetary administration offices located in the Alps. "This is not a decision we can make on our own."

"I have," said George, "and they're tending to take the hard line on this – rights of law and precedent, all that sort of thing." He grimaced. "We may end up at war no matter what we do."

"Well, they will be polling the individual bathospheres for our vote, won't they?"

George Alexander shook his head from side to side. "Not yet. They've decided to wait to see if in fact the Martians do initiate hostile action."

The meeting disintegrated into chaos, as the members fell to talking amongst themselves.

"... at last we can get rid of those stupid gladiator games on 3D," said Maisy Moor, Minister of Internal Affairs and Security. Her post had been created after the war, when the council decided that they needed someone to act as intermediary between the human population and the policing clones.

"... the economy will expand ..." said Richard Greenwood, Minister of International Relations.

"How, if we end up under embargo from the primary mineral-producing planet?" snapped the Minister of Industry and Finance, Ted Wade.

"How are our supplies of minerals and silicates?" said Barrymore-Smythe.

"Sufficient for our current manufacturing needs," said Wade. "If, however, we need to swing into full wartime production, especially of ships, there'll be shortages. If what you say is true, George, it's too late to stock up now, although I could get my Lunar agents to procure contracts with the major mining concerns," Wade asserted.

"And what if the Moon follows the Martian example?"

"Disaster, total disaster," breathed George Alexander. "I can tell you that as Minister of Food Distribution."

"What? I thought our stores were full," said Germaine Austin.

"They are, but as always we hang in a precarious balance. Should anything interrupt the continuous food shipments between Earth and the Moon, we're lost." He shivered.

Murti returned to the only issue upon which they must act quickly. "What about the *Revenant* and her passengers? What do we do about her?"

Richard Greenwood spoke. "The esteemed head of DSHQ should be here to report on that." The department of international relations was also newly created.

George blushed furiously. "They have been informed of the declaration, but not its cause, and told to dawdle as long as possible. They will proceed under normal propulsion using the slowest possible speed while we", he paused to clear his throat, "pursue diplomatic channels of negotiation."

"Yes, what about that?" said Murti. "Can't we just rescind the Lilliputian land grant? If we do that, then there's no dispute."

"And what of the clones?" George asked stiffly.

"All right, so we grant different, unoccupied land this time."

"They could still protest our right to grant land. Besides, it's gone beyond that point," said

Barrymore-Smythe. "The grant may have been the catalyst, but it's not the issue, not any more. They want freedom, independence. Nothing less will do," said Barrymore-Smythe.

"But the Alliance!" said Moor.

"And precedence!" interjected Greenwood.

"Means nothing if you're freezing your carcass scraping hoarfrost on the Martian pole, or digging up silicates on the planet surface, or grappling meteors from the sky for their mineral content," said George. "It's a brave new world out there, and we've done precious little to help them."

Barrymore-Smythe cut in: "Meanwhile, I believe it might be in order, Ted, if you were to follow up on the idea of a mineral agreement with the Moon. How are we doing on food, George?"

"All our reserves have been irradiated, so what stores we have should keep. I'll get my representatives to purchase enough to refill those storage facilities we have depleted and see if I can step up hydroponic production here on Earth, while my people look for additional bunkers. If", he added gloomily, "someone else hasn't got there first. Every island and bathosphere complex on Earth is facing the same predicament, and they're probably mobilizing their agents already."

Barrymore-Smythe clapped his hands together. "Good. It looks like we have our work cut out for us then. We'd best get started."

"What about recruitment?" said Maisy.

Barrymore-Smythe raised his hands in a gesture of denial. "Please, don't anticipate a draft. Let's hope we can negotiate. If the need arises, security is your domain. You have the facilities available and the procedures already set up. Recruitment would fall under your authority."

"I'll prepare, sir."

"As you wish. I think that's it for now. This council is now dissolved. Everyone go to your respective offices and consider how you can best prepare for war. Place your staff in a state of alert and readiness. We will reconvene tomorrow to co-ordinate activities – unless something comes up and we need to gather earlier. We will keep you posted on any developments or any pronouncements from Central, on the 1A Security line."

"What about the media?" Norm Bandy, head of water and the environment, stared straight at George as he spoke.

"The memo was directed to DSHQ, or the old Galactic War Headquarters, as it would be," said Barrymore-Smythe. "As far as we know no news has been released to the media by the Martian territorial government, and certainly not by ours. They remain in blissful ignorance, unless we have a leak."

Everyone faced George.

"What about your wife?" Schwartz enquired.

"I have not seen my wife. I would assume that

Jennifer is at BAND offices doing her job, just as I am here doing mine," George said brusquely.

"The media will be informed strictly on a need-to-know basis," said Barrymore-Smythe. "Since Earth has yet to draw up her formal response, there is so far no news to report."

"Right, just a small matter of war," said Sonya Freedman, head of technology.

"War contingent upon our taking hostile action. As long as we've taken no action, it's not official yet.

"Shall we adjourn?" said the chief. "All except George and Minister Moor. If you both could stay for a moment." He nodded to the security minister. "Please wait outside. I need to speak to George privately."

The council members shuffled from the room. George stood, hands stuffed in his pockets, and stared at the floor.

"I'm worried about Dirk. Don't you think we should start looking for him?"

"It's just a childish tantrum. He's upset because his friends have left, and I gather there's been a tiff with his girlfriend too. He's just a kid."

"Are you so sure? If you'd asked me last night during the party, I would have agreed with you, but not today. He takes his responsibilities seriously. You know that as well as I do. He may have missed the unofficial party last night in a fit of pique, but not today's ceremony, and certainly not this meeting."

George Alexander took off his spectacles and polished them, scowling.

"Don't forget we don't know how long the Martians have been planning this action. They've known about the land grant for a few months, so they have had time to assimilate the information and organize accordingly. As head of DSHQ – and hero of the Galactic Conflict – Dirk would be the most likely target for a terrorist attack or an abduction."

A furrow appeared on George's forehead.

"Have you seen him at all today?"

"Come to think of it, no. I looked into his room and he was gone. I just thought he'd left early to say a private farewell."

"Sounds reasonable. I probably would have assumed the same thing. But if that had been the case, then he would have appeared at the ceremony and the meeting."

Barrymore-Smythe pressed a button on the table and Maisy Moor's dark face filled the wall screen. "Ms Moor, would you please come in?"

The door retracted into the wall. "Yes, sir?"

"I would like to implement a search for our young Dirk." He glanced at George. "Discreetly, of course – no point in getting people up in arms about what may be nothing more than a childish fit of temper. Still, I'd like you to start enquiries right away."

"Should I contact the Lilliputian ship?"

"No, he's logged on to his computer," said

George. "That means he's still somewhere in the facility. Perhaps he's hiding out. Try the clones' quarters."

Ms Moor gave George a sidelong glance. "Aye, aye, sir."

She saluted, spun on her heel and strode from the room.

As the door to DSHQ whooshed shut behind her, a distraught man with red hair and flushed face rushed up to Ms Moor and plucked at her sleeve.

"Do you have a moment?" he said, twisting his cap in his hands. "I need to talk to you about my daughter, Gwen."

Gwen extricated herself from the crawlspace with a wriggle and a squirm and lifted herself on to her hands and knees. Her head creaked on her neck and her spine popped as she twisted to peer at the bend where clones had vanished.

This was ridiculous. The Manta-class vessel was riddled with maintenance passages, and Gwen knew from her experiences at the orbital that she could easily cross from one end of the ship to the other without ever entering the public corridors. Why was she dawdling here?

Because every time she made good her escape someone else approached. She squatted, ready to jump.

What she needed was a map so she could find the nearest entrance.

There should be a terminal close at hand. Gwen had been trying to reach it all afternoon, but kept getting chased into some cubbyhole or another to wait until crew members passed. By now she knew every storage closet, niche, alcove and vent in this sector of the ship.

She chided herself; she should've known better than to head for engineering, but the ratio of computer stations per linear metre was greater here than anywhere else on the ship, outside the bridge.

The girl straightened up and dusted herself off. The blood flowed back into her feet, warming them. She rubbed her face with her hands and marched down the corridor to the computer.

"Here you are!" Gwen cried. "Now let's see what we can find." She knelt at the terminal, which had been installed at a Lilliputian height, and keyed in her passcode and query. Then she took a compu-cube, a voice-activated palm-sized system with a holograph screen, from her pocket.

At least she had the presence of mind to bring this. She pulled a wire from around her waist and hooked the cube to the mainframe.

"Download all schematics of maintenance corridors, ventilation shafts, electrical conduits. Now what else do I need?" She tapped her tooth in an unconscious imitation of Dirk.

"That ought to do it for now," she murmured to herself, "and these things have only so much memory, you know."

She clapped her hand over her mouth. Here only five hours and she was starting to talk to herself.

The computer beeped.

FILE COPIES COMPLETE, ANOTHER?

"No, thank you," she said as she disconnected the cube from the main frame. "Open maintenance corridor schematic." A 3D image of the ship minus the solidity of walls or outer hull drifted in front of her face.

"All right!" she exclaimed. "That's more like it!"

"What was that? Who's there?" someone shouted.

Gwen swore. The nearest entrance to the maintenance ramp was some 28 metres away – too far. Her hair flew as she looked frantically about for an exit, any exit. The voices drew near.

Gwen ran and dived back into the same crawl-space from which she had emerged. As she scrambled to turn around in the tight space, she cracked her head against the ceiling. Tears started to her eyes. She whimpered and bit her tongue to smother all sound, but a small cry escaped her lips.

"Did you hear that?"

"Hear what?"

Two pairs of feet stopped outside her hideaway. "I don't know ... something."

"You're imagining things, and we've got work to do."

The feet tramped on, moving beyond her range of vision, and the voices faded.

"Computer," she whispered, "open maintenance schematics." The skeletal outline of the ship floated eerily half in and half out of the wall. She traced the outline from the nearest entrance deeper into the belly of the ship. She wanted to avoid the living quarters, flanked by kitchen and sanitation facilities. Not that she wouldn't need access to both, but she reasoned that apart from the bridge and the engineering section, the living quarters would be the most trafficked area of the ship, therefore best bypassed whenever possible. Cargo holds, particularly those designated for Deep Space stores, would be the least frequented.

Her finger stabbed a spot on the opposite side of the craft, as far from here as possible. It meant she would have to walk a long way to obtain her meals, but it wasn't as though she had anything better to do.

Gwen would want computer access too. "Enlarge sector G3, magnification 100 times. Insert walls. I'm looking for areas of dead or wasted space behind walls, preferably near a terminal."

The appropriate section swelled. A dizzying assortment of lines appeared, solidified. As the compu-cube scanned the layout, different rooms and bays lit up, until one blinked red.

"Fantastic! Save that and close file."

The image vanished. She pocketed the cube before poking her head into the corridor.

The girl held her breath and listened for a minute. Then she clambered from her hiding-place, scurried up the hall towards the nearest maintenance portal and disappeared into the shaft.

1/9/2334

Twenty-hundred Hours

"H e's just sulking, that's all," said George for the umpteenth time that day.

Jennifer Alexander frowned at her husband. "I don't understand your attitude. Don't you think you're being a little bit hard on the boy?"

George shrugged.

"Have you contacted the ship?" said Jennifer.

"What ship?"

"The *Revenant*, of course."

George averted his gaze from his reporter wife. "Ah, no, not about that." He glanced up. "But Dirk has logged on to the computer to retrieve his messages, so he must be somewhere in the facility."

"Why do you say that? Do you remember who we're discussing?" Mr Alexander opened his mouth, but Jennifer Alexander forged ahead. "This is Dirk, the same Dirk who broke into the top-secret military software and revealed the war for what it was, a lie. The same Dirk who dug into AWS's memory banks to discover the secret of star drive."

George sputtered. "I'm aware—"

"I don't think you are. This is our son who cut his teeth on computers, who spent more time hacking than playing. Do you think that it would be at all difficult for him to write a macro that would log him on and dump his messages in order to cover his tracks?"

"Well. . ." George elongated the word, as if it were being drawn from him reluctantly.

"Honestly, George, I don't think you give him half the credit he deserves. You know as well as I do that such a program would be a snap to him – mere child's play," Jennifer concluded. "If you don't contact the *Revenant*, I will."

George Alexander couldn't let that happen. If his wife talked to the Lilliputian clones, word about the declaration of war would get out.

"I'll call them." He conceded defeat, but his wife brushed past him and spoke to the computer. "AWS, open a comm-line to the *Revenant II*."

"I'm sorry the council has ordered all channels to spa—"

"Belay that, AWS, this is council member George Alexander, Minister of Food Distribution."

The computer was silent as it absorbed the information.

"What's going on? Why have the council—"

George cut in, "They don't want the Lilliputian ship besieged by well-wishers."

"But—"

The computer came back on-line. "Communication channel open."

A video sprang to life, and the face of communications specialist Ylon filled the screen.

"Ylon! Good. Just the person I wanted to speak to," said George.

Jennifer Alexander scrutinized her husband's face. He was keeping something from her. She elbowed him out of the way. "Ylon, have you seen Dirk?"

An atmosphere of subdued alarm permeated the ship. Even separated from the rest of the crew, the repercussions of DSHQ's directive and the urgency it generated carried through to the bridge.

With the vessel filled near to bursting, the crew were forced to revert to the rigours of old war days. Living quarters were assigned in shifts of eight hours, as the former sleep cradles had been, and still it was not enough room to house a population five times its normal size.

Housekeeping droids scurried in a state of controlled panic, or the nearest that mechanoids could muster, as every nook, cranny or cubbyhole was converted to a potential sleeping space. Water would have to be severely rationed while portions of food were cut. Those department heads most affected queued to consult with the captain.

"No, Sergeant," said Zed, "I don't think we can contact the Moon for additional supplies. I think the less people are aware of our progress the better. Although DSHQ hasn't said anything, the timing of the declaration and the way it coincides with the arrival of our passengers is a little too convenient. I suspect it is our presence that has precipitated this crisis. We already know from past experience that the Lunar colonies are ripe for rebellion, and they have reason to resent us for our participation in the last controversy. Who knows where they will choose to ally themselves in this battle?"

The mess-sergeant mumbled something.

"We'll just have to make do with short rations. Talk to the production manager in hydroponics and see if they can force some of the produce to ripen early."

The captain glowered at Ylon as he caught him eavesdropping.

The communications officer turned to stare at the blank console. Since the captain had ordered silent running – standard operating procedure in a combat situation – he had little to do. He ran the standard checks twice. Blast calibrated and recalibrated the satellite's position to ensure they would be in continuous contact with Earth, ready for any important messages or orders, but Ylon didn't expect any. He'd lived long enough on Earth to realize it would take a while for humanity to awaken to the crisis.

So Ylon was almost knocked off his chair when the comm-unit tweedled in his ear. He was even more surprised when the face of George Alexander filled the comm-link screen.

Before the Lilliputian clone had a chance to speak, Jennifer Alexander came barging into the conversation.

"Ylon, have you seen Dirk?"

Behind her, her spouse was frantically waving his hands, shaking his head in negation and mouthing something – the only word of which Ylon recognized was "no".

Blast cast a sidelong glance at Ylon. He leaned back in his chair and exhaled slowly. Evidently, the councils had yet to inform the public of the Martian declaration.

Her next statement floored him. "Dirk seems to be missing."

He jumped out of his seat. "What?"

"You wouldn't happen to have talked to him?"

"No, I'm sorry, Mrs Alexander. He didn't attend either the ceremony or the party last night."

"I didn't mean then. I was thinking more, um, er, recently." She stammered to a halt as if she didn't know what to say next.

It took a while before it hit Ylon exactly what she

was trying to say or, more precisely, not say. Jennifer Alexander thought that he and Blast had spirited the young Dirk aboard the *Revenant*.

The reply was forming on his lips when a hand clenched his shoulder hard.

"What's this, Lieutenant, a personal call? I thought I'd ordered silent running."

"Silent running?" interjected Dirk's mother.

"Mrs and Mr Alexander, how may we help you?" Captain Zed's gaze slid from the mother to the gesticulating father.

"Isn't that the final stage before battle?"

The captain's eyes glazed and he forced a wooden smile to his lips. "Just an exercise. We have been on Earth many months now and we are out of practice. Mustn't let the crew get flabby. Who knows what we'll confront in the next galaxy?"

Apparently satisfied by his explanation, Jennifer Alexander returned to the topic that was foremost on her mind – her son.

Captain and concerned mother conferred for a few moments, and the link was severed.

"Lieutenant, you are dismissed from the commpanel. Blast, you're in charge here for a while. Ylon, I want you to organize a search. We've got more than enough people. Grab some of the passengers. It'll put them to good use and give them something to do. You and your partner here," he indicated Blast with a jut of his thumb, "know the lad better than anyone else, but I can't spare both of you. Someone must mind the shop. You know how he thinks and what he's likely to do. See if you can find him."

"It'll take time. It's a big ship."

"We've got plenty of time till we get to Mars; but if he's here, we must find him before we reach our destination. If the search lasts beyond this day, then we can arrange two-shifts between yourself and your cohort here. There won't be much for you to do as long as we are maintaining radio silence. Let's just hope we don't get too many more pressing calls."

Orders given, Zed swung away from the clones, muttering. "I think we've had more than enough emergencies for one day."

George deflated like an empty balloon as the screen went blank. Jennifer gave her husband a long and searching look before pushing away from the vid-phone.

She swept her hand across the plasti-glas screen and rubbed her fingers together. A crease formed between her brows.

"Robbie," she called.

"What's wrong?"

"Dust."

George Alexander burst out laughing.

"What's so funny?"

"Nothing."

"Robbie!" She stood. "Where is he?"

"Robbie?"

"Yes, Robbie – funny little square robot that does most of the housework."

"I know who Robbie is," George snarled. "I can't say I've seen him, but then I haven't been looking. I suppose he's trundling around some place."

Jennifer poked her head into their bedroom and then Dirk's. "No, he's definitely not here. I wonder ..." she turned her gaze upon her husband "... if Dirk and Robbie have both gone."

"Do you think they're together?" said George.

She headed back to the vid-phone. "I should contact the ship."

He intercepted her. "If Dirk and Robbie are together, the crew'll find them."

Dirk sat on the bedroll, stuck his legs out experimentally and immediately stubbed his toe against a box. He rose, scratching his head.

Something was not right. He should have enough leg room.

Dirk had been meticulous in his measurements, both in choosing his location and in laying in his supplies, for he had wanted a single base to which he could retreat. There had been a lot to bring, what with food and supplies enough to make life comfortable for an indefinite period of time. And he did not want his things to expand beyond the boundaries of his room.

Also he needed the lighting provided by the radiant floorboards. Therefore the fewer packages he had to block out the low-level illumination in his living area, the better. Still, open cartons lined all four walls. Of course, each work space had an intensity switch, but Dirk could not afford to use them often, for such a continuous energy drain in an allegedly unoccupied portion of the vessel would be noticed.

Dirk stared at the thin line of light between the row of boxes and the wall.

Something had been moved. He was sure of it.

That box wasn't flush against the wall as it should have been, but skewed with a corner jutting out as though it had been jostled.

The youth glowered at the offending article. Something or someone had moved it. Dirk knew *he* hadn't touched it.

A cat's paw of fear brushed his neck.

Dirk groped for the old-style oil lamp he had brought from home. Bless his mum and her fascination with antiques. Her collection, picked up in auction, had provided him with some items, like the lamp, that would have been impossible to come across elsewhere. He felt a pang of guilt which he swiftly suppressed.

He patted his pockets for matches. The lamp had been easy, thanks to his mum, but the matches were another matter. He had had to have them specially made.

Dirk struck the phosphorous tip against the abrasive board.

The match sparked and flared.

The lamp was plain and unadorned, a single cup with a spout and a wick. According to his mum, it was Roman, dating back to a time before the Flood, before the Exodus, before Britain had been a nation, before even the fabled Arthur had tried to turn a group of petty kingdoms into a nationstate.

It was a simple enough affair. A cupped bowl held oil, with a ring. The wick was draped across the vessel, soaking up the oil.

Dirk held the match to the wick, still dubious that this thing would work. The fire lapped at the wick and it flamed. He raised the lamp above his head and peered in the gloom, marvelling that people had once used these to light their homes.

Shadows danced and leapt, and for a while it seemed the room came alive around him. The table vaulted into focus and retreated back into darkness. He cupped his hand around the flame and lowered the lamp. Then he made a circuit around the cubicle.

Not one but all of the boxes had been moved a few centimetres away from the wall, as if somebody had needed to get behind them to the panels beyond.

What was this? Dirk crouched down and snatched a piece of string from the floor – the same kind of cord he had used to tie up the boxes in the storage area. As the things he had in the living area were in continuous use, he hadn't bothered to bind any of those cartons.

He jumped up, stalked to the storage room and thrust the lamp through the door. The wick slid into the oil. The flame went out. He stopped, fumbled with both wick and match and relit it.

Then Dirk bent to examine the knots on the top of each carton and gasped.

Somebody or something had been here, all right. Someone with a tidiness fetish. Dirk had been slip-shod with his knots, but someone – or something – had retied them in meticulous bows with measured strands and loops of 10 centimetres. Someone had even trimmed the frayed ends on each string.

The skin on his neck did a slow creep as he surveyed his sanctuary. It no longer felt safe to him. No doubt about it, someone had discovered his lair.

Gwen wiped her hands on her trousers and stepped back to appraise her work. She'd come to the ship quite unprepared, not even sure what she was going to do until she had done it.

The idea of stealing aboard ship came to her at the party. Her father had stood detached and remote in the corner of the room, and the conversation with Ylon and Blast had lagged as they kept casting oblique glances at the door, looking for Dirk.

When Gwen acted, she acted on impulse. She should have planned, but there was only enough time to return to their temporary groundside quarters, grab her bag, and go. With the first revving of the engines, it became too late to go back.

Even now, she couldn't've explained what she was doing or why. She only knew that she had to get away. She was tired of being the daughter of the recently demoted Perry Finn. Even though she had been absolved of all guilt, she still felt the shame acutely. And she was tired of seeing pity in people's eyes – especially Dirk's. She had started to avoid him, not knowing what to say. The more she avoided him the less she could find to say, until the gulf between them had become too great.

Right or wrong, the decision was made. She had left Earth as she had left Dirk behind. She couldn't wander out to the crew and say, "Gee whiz! I've made a mistake."

Somehow, she'd have to make a go of it, but she'd have to think creatively to do so.

Gwen had brought only one bag with her, the same bag that was supposed to do for a weekend trip groundside to watch the launch. She had two standard jumpsuits, and another – more dressy – which she had brought for the party.

She had had to scrounge among the cargo bays to come up with something to make a home. With their nice assortment of crates, the initial temptation had been to set up house in one of the cargo bays, rather than the dead space the computer had pinpointed inside a hollow bulkhead; but when Gwen had measured the space, she decided this would do.

Although Gwen should not have been surprised, she was dismayed when she realized that everything – from blankets to furnishings – was of Lilliputian proportions.

One of their tables made a respectable stool, or six laid end to end made a reasonable bed stand. She'd used crates to complete the "suite" after checking the labels to make sure they didn't contain hazardous materials. A larger box marked "Tents" made a table, and a smaller one worked as a chair once Gwen pushed it against the wall to provide a backrest.

She'd ordered blankets until the computer cut her off. It would take three to cover her from head to toe, and then she would forever be fussing with them unless she could cobble them together somehow. Gwen recollected her mother had told her once about an ancient art, originating from the time before machines could weave a suit as a single cloth, called sewing. The girl gave a mirthless snigger. Wonderful, she thought, as if she was going to learn how to sew.

Then she had been forced to pilfer clean replacement uniforms from the laundry to make a mattress. The makeshift berth looked more like a pile of linen than a bed. She'd be lucky if she didn't get tangled and choke herself to death in her sleep.

"A couple of holos and this place would be

lovely." Gwen laughed out loud, and flinched at the hollow sound of her voice inside the metal bulkhead.

Lowering her voice, she mumbled, "Be it ever so humble..."

Her stomach growled. "All right, all right, all right, I'll feed you. But first..."

Pinching a fold of her clothing she brought it up to her nose. How long could she make her two outfits last? She sniffed and pursed her lips.

Not long.

She grabbed the only clean suit she had left and changed clothes. Eventually, she would have to order something from the computer, but not yet, not so soon in the voyage, for such an act might reveal her presence to the clones.

She slung the dirty jumpsuit over her shoulder. At least she could use the laundry facilities to wash not only her clothes, but also her person.

Again her stomach rumbled in complaint. She had not eaten since the party and it was long past dinner. Gwen flopped into her makeshift chair and spoke to the compu-cube. "Kitchens."

The cube, the room's only adornment, immediately provided a 3D display of the ship.

"Easiest route," she hesitated, amending her statement, "using the ventilation shafts and maintenance corridors. Something I can walk through. Dimensions: height 175 cm. Width," she considered for a minute, "one metre." She wanted to be able to turn around.

A snaking line appeared.

"Great." She stuffed the cube in her overalls. "I guess I'd better take you with me until I learn the route." Then she scooped the empty bag from the floor. She could drop the other suit off on the way.

The kitchens were busy, as she might have expected after dinner, but they were crowded with Lilliputian clones, not droids.

She squeezed her body against the wall and strained to hear.

What was up?

Suddenly it dawned on her what had been bothering her since her arrival on the ship – something noted as a part of the background noise so typical of space flight that it did not seem amiss, so it was set aside for later examination after she'd satisfied her preliminary needs for food and lodgings.

The engines. They were using standard propulsion engines, and now that she thought about it, by her reckoning of time they should have reached Mars by now, had they leapt as planned.

Two clones drew near her position, just inside the vent.

"We should have enough," a young aide said soothingly. "We have the stores to last us until the edge of the galaxy."

"Yes, assuming we took normal scheduled leaps to

Mars, but we're not, and we have to feed five times the normal contingent until we get there."

The mess-sergeant clasped his hands behind his back and paced up and down. "It's unlikely we'll be able to replenish our food supplies there, assuming we are lucky enough to unload our passengers."

The mess-sergeant pivoted, heading straight for Gwen. The aide scrambled to keep up with him.

"Take notes, please. We'll need to reprogram the droids. If we cut portions by one-third we will still be within the minimum dietary allowance of calories. Remind me to contact the ship's surgeon for a dietary supplement."

They advanced upon her. Gwen backed into a refrigerator. Absentmindedly she plucked an apple from a crate and munched on it. So, she had been right. They were proceeding to Mars under normal power and – the apple caught in her throat – remained unsure of their reception there.

The mess-sergeant and the quartermaster advanced upon the refrigerator. The door began to open. Her head swung from side to side.

She ducked behind a slab of beef.

The Lilliputs moved up and down the rows of shelves and food, counting. She listened, hoping to glean further information about their predicament, but the clones kept to their inventory.

They drew near to her hiding-place, and she shuffled around the side of beef, keeping it between herself and the clones. It brushed against her in a chilling embrace and some of the blood rubbed off, forming scarlet crystals on her skin.

A shiver shook her body and she slipped from one slab of meat to another. They switched to another row. Gwen blew on her hands and examined her nails – they were turning blue. She was losing the feeling in her fingers and toes. She stamped her feet.

"What was that?"

"Pay attention to what you're doing. I'd like to get out of here before we freeze to death," snapped the sergeant.

Gwen silently cheered the sentiment as she clasped her arms around herself and performed a little jig to keep warm.

"There's..." The aide rattled off a number.

Gwen jumped up and down. "Hu-hu-hu-hurry!" she chattered.

"Yes, I think we can stretch this to last for two meals, if seconds are denied and rations cut. Very good. Let's get out of here."

Gwen followed the voices to the door, with a strange shuffle, hop, shiver. When the two clones had left, she spun, stuffing apples, fresh fruit and cheeses into her bag. She peered through the frosty window, her breath creating little icicle patterns on the glass.

She emerged from the fridge and began grabbing anything she could lay her hands on. Bread, nuts, cakes, crisps – anything she wouldn't have to cook.

When the bag was full, she stuffed food into her pockets, her shirt, even up her sleeves.

Again voices intruded on her consciousness.

"Wait a second," said the mess-sergeant. "Didn't we have three of those just five minutes ago?"

And Gwen fled, rattling and clanging as she went.

There was a splutter of exasperation behind her. "Don't tell me, let me guess. One of the drones is on the fritz."

The first Martian councils were disorganized affairs, and Gordon Rhys wore the mantle of leadership uneasily. For here in the fringes of space, no one man, nor governmental body, had ever ruled. The former colonial administration was a sham, its officials dusted off for dinner parties and ribbon-cutting ceremonies, neither of which Mars had in abundance.

The Martian colony had had no military, no law force to speak of, no laws. Such laws as they had had varied from dominion to dominion, and each dominion had been made by an individual who had carved it from the planet's breast – an individual who made rules on a whim, broke them just as readily, and enforced them as it suited.

It was this lack of co-ordinated effort in the past that hampered them now as each captain put forth suggestions and refused to listen to any others.

Gordon Rhys scowled. The Martians were only

marginally more prepared than Earth for this conflict, and his note of caution was not well received.

Yet it was this same lawlessness that made it necessary to arm all Martian ships. Thus, Mars had *something* that resembled a fleet. However, few Martian vessels were constructed for the sustained flight to Earth. Little more than runabouts, the ships had only the fuel capacity for the passage between Mars and the two moons, Diemos and Phobos. Passenger transport was run by the Alliance, leaving only those cargo carriers and merchants that made the regular junket to the Moon with the engine capacity to go the distance required.

"We are agreed then?" *On something. Finally*, he thought, but dared not verbalize. The elected leader Rhys surveyed his fellow council members. "To wait and take aggressive action when the *Revenant* arrives."

There were grumbles all around.

"And since we do not have the capability to take the war to their own sphere, then we have only one alternative: all our forces must be marshalled to patrol Martian space. We will hunt down the Lilliputian ship and seize it. Make it our own. Then Earth's top technology will belong to us."

"Aye" ... "Aye" ... "Aye" ... "Aye" ...

Cheers reverberated in the rafters of the room, drowning out the rest of his words about treating their Lilliputian guests with respect.

2/9/2334

Twelve-hundred Hours

"What in heaven's name is that?" The *Revenant's* second-shift Chief Technical Officer Proto pointed at a piece of cloth that hung across the wall like a curtain. It fluttered in the breeze of a nearby ventilation shaft. He marched forward.

The curtain rattled and rustled. He stopped, amazed. Then the officer thrust the cloth aside to expose a dull metal box, quite another colour from the rest of the hall. He opened the compartment door and gaped at the computer terminal inside.

"This isn't on the blueprints," he said to his assistant.

"Maybe they forgot."

"Unlikely, but not impossible," said Proto. "Make

note of it, and we'll add it to the inventory. Later we can come back and do the programming."

"Why the drape, I wonder? And why here of all places?" queried his assistant, Corpman Psi.

The technical officer thrust out his lower lip and tugged at it. His head swept slowly from side to side. "Don't know. Maybe one of the people at refit decided to add their own personal mark to their handiwork."

The young corpman wrinkled her nose scornfully. "Floral. It must be somebody's idea of a joke."

"Still, nice to know there's an additional terminal here. We can always remove the curtain."

Psi moved to act upon his suggestion, and the cloth quivered violently.

"Later," Proto amended. "We've got to finish searching this sector before fourteen-hundred hours. Come on. Let's see if we can find our young stow-away..."

Robbie tarried a few minutes before bolting from its niche, until the heat-activated sensor images of the two Lilliputian crew were faded to a nice blue by the separating bulkheads.

Blend right in, ha!

The servo-mech trembled indignantly.

Discovered within forty-eight hours, and the inactivity had not worn well. Programmed to assist, the servo-mechanism had felt obliged to check on Dirk twice and, since it had just happened to be there, dusting, hoovering, and generally tidying up the place.

Shut down. That's what AWS had said. Foolishness.

In Robbie's thirty years of service to the Alexanders, the servo-mech had never been turned off, and it wasn't about to start now. Besides, if the robot hadn't been awake and alert, the two of them might very well have been taken in for reprogramming. At the very least, Robbie would have lost his drape.

The servo-mech rolled back and forth in agitation, torn between running to escape or hastening to Dirk to warn him of the Lilliputians' search, but that would mean disclosing his presence to his young master. The robot quickly abandoned the idea. To reach Dirk Robbie would have to get past the clones, drawing attention not only to the servo-mech but more importantly to the youth. Far better to draw the Lilliputs away if possible.

And Robbie put his plan into action, rotating one-hundred-and-eighty degrees to race squealing up the maintenance corridor.

Proto and Psi scowled at the schematic display.

"I don't see any place to hide," said Psi.

Proto contradicted his aide. "There's a maintenance closet for the vacuum system to the living quarters some hundred metres up and to the right."

Squeak, squeak, squeak.

Proto stared up the hall.

Squeak, squeak, squeak.

"What is that?" The commander tensed. "Corpman, follow that racket. We may have found our intruder."

Psi sprinted down the hall, with Proto at his heels. They careered around the next corner, their headlong rush arrested when they saw the hole previously covered by floral drape.

"The terminal cabinet is missing," rasped Psi.

"Impossible! Terminals don't pick up and walk away."

Squeak, squeak, squeak.

They swung towards the sound. "That way. After it!"

Psi bolted and the older Proto shambled after her. She skidded into an adjacent corridor and collided with a droid wearing, of all things, an apron.

"Ah! A housekeeping droid," Proto wheezed as he bent over, trying to catch his breath. "That explains the apron."

"What's a housekeeping droid doing down here? Dusting?"

"Must be a reserve."

The two fanned out, approaching the servomechanism from either side as if corralling a skittish horse. The box shuddered, rolling this way and that.

"What is it doing with a terminal in its belly?" mused Psi.

"Maybe it's an upgrade. I can't say I've spent much time with the housekeeping units they've installed in the *Revenant*." The CTO patted the box.

It juddered and shook.

"Poor thing," said Proto. "It doesn't seem to be in the best of shape."

The robot clattered so loud that it appeared about to unhinge itself.

Proto pushed the droid gently and lovingly forward. Robbie hummed. A wheel creaked.

"Needs oiling." He pulled it back. "Take this thing back to repair for servicing."

"What about the search?"

The engineer glared back over his shoulder. "With the amount of noise this thing is making, if there was anyone hiding anywhere along this hall, they're long gone by now."

His comm-unit whistled shrilly. The officer flinched, rolling his eyes heavenwards.

"Oh, that's great! Just in case our quarry hasn't heard us yet." He indicated the quaking droid with a rap on its metal exterior.

The comm-unit cracked. "Kgggh-*Brz-burble*-Communications Specialist Ylon, here. Any luck, Commander?"

"This sector appears to be clean, although we have stumbled across a housekeeping droid that seems to have got lost. We were just getting ready to take it in for a good servicing."

"Send your assistant. Your presence is requested in the wardroom in five minutes."

"You heard what the man said. Take the droid in for repairs. Check the terminal. See what software it's got running and what sort of use we can put it to. We'll have to finish this portion later."

Corpman Psi saluted and then whirled smartly. She considered the quivering robot.

"Oh, stop rattling," she said, "unless you want to end up on the scrap heap."

It froze mid-clang. She gawped at it. The average housekeeping droid had a vocabulary limited to its function – words like fetch, carry, wash and clean. This thing shouldn't have been able to understand her threat.

Neither should it react.

Psi stooped slightly until she was on "eye" level with it. She stared into the photoreceptor and regarded her own slightly inflated and inverted reflection in the convex lens.

"Well," she said, "you also heard what the man said. Let's go."

The concept of insubordination in a droid was inconceivable, so she straightened and started down the hall without a second glance, secure in the knowledge that the servo-mech would follow.

Robbie went into the robotic equivalent of a convulsion. *Rattle! Clatter! Crash!*

Its photoreceptor cells rolled in their sockets. To resist a direct order would be impossible, and it would only serve to call attention to itself, inviting a complete memory wipe.

So Robbie complied with a slight elevation of twin retractor arms, a motion not unlike a person throwing up his hands in dismay while its metal mind whirred.

Robbie tried to formulate some sort of plan. Connected as it was to the larger computer, the servo-mech had access to AWS's memory banks. It riffled through a series of line drawings until it found the one that it wanted – a map of the *Revenant*.

The human (all people, both Lilliputian and large, looked alike to Robbie) had only said let's go. She didn't say that the robot had to stay. Perhaps, when they made it to another part of the ship, Robbie could sneak away.

Squeak. Squeak. Squeak.

A noisier part of the ship. Robbie cocked a non-existent ear and revised his plans.

"I sometimes wonder what sort of junk they saddled us with," Psi complained.

The servo-mech whistled querulously.

"Wouldn't be at all surprised if this boat fell apart half-in and half-out of ultra-space," the technician grumbled. "It'd be just like the big people."

The corpman ducked through a portal into the occupied portion of the vessel.

Psi took Robbie up a level. They entered the living quarters through which they must travel to get to the working part of the ship.

The corridors were swarming with people. Lilliputian clones, both in uniform and not, and droids dashed here and there, in some sort of ordered chaos. Searchers were poking into cupboards and cabinets while passengers and sleeping shift crew members were dragged from their beds to line the hall three abreast while their rooms were searched.

The noise factor increased to a crescendo, from orderly rumble to tumultuous din, as Psi shouldered her way through the throng with the screeching Robbie in her wake. The robot pulled back.

A hand clasped a rotor-arm. "Good! A servo-mech. Just what we needed."

And Robbie was propelled into one of the cubicles. "Here, take this." The searcher dumped a pile of clothes on the servo-mech's back and glared at the female passenger. "To the cargo bay. We don't have room for this here."

She squawked, "Hey! I'm going to need those things on Mars, and we were told there was no weight restrictions since we were supposed to jump and disembark in a matter of minutes. How was I supposed to know that we wouldn't?"

The officer softened his tone. "None of us did, but we are pressed for space and don't have room for these items if others have to share the same quarters."

Robbie swung from side to side as it followed the conversation.

"I don't want to be separated from my things."

"I will give you a receipt for them."

Mollified, the passenger relaxed, and Robbie was released from service. Heaped with clothes, it trundled out of the door and shoved its way back the way it had come.

Squeak ... *thud* ... "Hey!" ... "Watch where you're going..."

The servo-mech settled next to a room marked "laundry". Blanketed with clothing, someone mistook it for a hamper, adding more to the pile. Twenty minutes later another person came by and obligingly replaced it in the closet where it belonged and shut the door behind it.

Psi had made it only a few metres up the hall when she noticed the droid was missing. She cursed volubly before keying her commander's code.

"I'm sorry, Commander, it's total anarchy here," she said, "and I seem to have lost the servo-mech."

Her report was met with a stunned silence so profound that the simple loss seemed to have more significance than she would have attached to it. She steeled herself for a dressing down.

His reply, when it came, was so mild, she sagged against the wall.

"Never mind. We have, ah, er, other priorities.

Report to the cargo bays where they are issuing weapons."

"Weapons, sir?"

"You have your orders, corpman. Now move."

"I say, if you're a leader, then lead. From home. Generals don't go charging about on the battlefield."

"Don't you see? I've got to go," Gordon Rhys argued with his wife. "The men are ripe for battle, and who knows what they'll do unless I'm there to oversee them. So far, Earth hasn't declared one way or another. Any premature military action could send them over the brink. I've got to be there to take command, to put the brakes on if nothing else."

Gordon Rhys Junior ruminated on what his parents said. Mars was at war and his father was going to lead them to battle against the Lilliputian ship. Young Rhys frowned. His room was littered with models – the Barracuda-style frigate, the Orca destroyer and Dolphin cruiser, along with the Piranha single-pilot fighter craft. He loved the military and would have loved to join the Centauri expedition force, if he weren't only six years old.

Now they were at war, and his father in command of the entire army. The boy's chest swelled with pride. He couldn't wait to tell his friend living on the colonies of the Moon, Tim. The child squirmed underneath the sheet, impatient for the dawn.

Chief Administrator Barrymore-Smythe fiddled with the items on his desk, straightening the many piles, aligning their corners to match perfectly the corners of the desk, then arranging and rearranging the stacks according to importance.

Quite honestly, the administrator didn't know what to do with himself. He'd already completed the mundane day-to-day minutiae of his office, initialling forms, checking orders, requisitions and inventory. All part of his daily routine. He sipped his morning cup of Kaffree stimulant.

Now what? With war looming on the horizon his duties of co-ordinating the many departments to keep the facility running smoothly seemed trivial.

The administrator examined the dregs in the bottom of the cup. Called guano, it supposedly derived from some vegetative substance that grew in the Amazons – although Barrymore-Smythe doubted it, since Brazil had been one of the first areas of land submerged during the Flood.

He picked up a dictionary, fingered the leather cover with pride (such luxuries were hard to come by) and leafed through the pages until he found the proper entry. His eyes swung from left to right.

Barrymore-Smythe took a final mouthful and ... spat.

"Bird-droppings!" he bellowed into the book.

Suddenly, the communications console that he had kept tuned to the DSHQ-line squawked, bursting to life with a roar of static and loud pop.

"Mayday! Mayday! This is Terran Carrier Nimrod ... *crackle* ... we have been just entered Martian space and have been fired upon by the Martian authorities..."

The reception was poor or perhaps the vessel had changed orientation, for the communication broke up. There were other noises, a whine or a drone followed by short, sharp reports, which Barrymore-Smythe recognized as weapons' fire.

What was the Nimrod doing in Martian space? He knew that they shouldn't have kept the declaration a secret.

Barrymore-Smythe jumped in his seat as the voice bellowed across the galaxy. "Mayday! Mayday! Lunar Control? Earth Control? DSHQ? Anybody? The Martian authorities have demanded we turn over this vessel. I repeat, they are in pursuit and have demanded we surrender this vessel or die..."

The communications ceased with a boom and a shriek, and the cup fell from nerveless fingers, soiling his nice tidy arrangement of stacks.

"Computer," the administrator's voice cracked, "locate each council member in their offices, in their homes, wherever they are, and have them report to me at DSHQ in twenty-five minutes."

"Cancel that." Another voice overrode his own, on his own comm-link too. Coloured dots swam across the vid-phone, coalescing to form the familiar features of the head of the central committee that saw to global affairs, Francis Willard. "We have already contacted them."

The administrator nodded as Willard made his announcement.

"At twelve-hundred hours today, the Martian colony committed the first official act of war. Since there has been a communications blackout for the past forty-eight hours, we may assume that this was not an isolated incident, but part of a concerted effort to seize Terran ships.

"In addition, news is coming in via financial channels that Earth's assets on Mars have been frozen, and possibly appropriated. In view of the emergency situation, we require an immediate vote."

Willard paused. "I see by the panel that the last of you have been located."

The head of the central global committee shuffled papers on his desk as the message from the cargo carrier Nimrod was repeated for any latecomers.

He stood. "As a result of this overt act of war, we can no longer afford to ignore the Martian rebels. We must respond. Either we accede to their demands or we meet force with force."

They replayed the message.

"We cannot make this sort of decision without

polling the council members of each and every facility. Due to the urgent nature of the situation, we require an emergency poll on the following proposal."

A declaration of war popped on to the screen, as the final explosion and scream was played over and over again.

Barrymore-Smythe ground his teeth. His head began to ache. When they called his name, he replied "Yea" before he had a chance to think about it.

Minutes dragged on. The administrator spun the volume control down, but it refused to respond. Evidently central command had set the level and locked it in.

Norm Bandy, Minister of Water and the Environment, was getting ready to sit on the toilet when the voice found him via his personal ear implant.

He fumed. The ear comm was supposed to be an unlisted number.

As they repeated the bulletin for the third time, he got the gist of the message even though he didn't have visual access to the written proposal.

He stormed from the stall. "Aye! Aye! Aye!" he roared when it was his time to vote. "Blow 'em outa the sky!"

George Alexander was up to his elbows in muck. Since the last food crisis, Dirk's father had become more and more interested in soil-based farming. He had allocated a certain portion of the quonset hut as a greenhouse of his own and smuggled in dirt from the surface. George came here when he needed to be alone to have time to think.

His face fell when the voice found him. He opened his mouth to protest, but his objections were muffled as they replayed the message.

"Minister of Food Distribution, Pennines District, George Alexander. Your vote, sir?"

George stared at the speaker he had rigged into his hideaway. "What, may I ask, is the proposal? I'm afraid I can't see it."

Some anonymous underling read the declaration.

"How many people have died on the ship?"

"I'm sorry, sir, I don't have that information. Your vote?"

"How many more are going to have to die before we learn?"

"Pardon?"

"I suppose the ayes have it."

"I really can't tell you that, sir. It might sway—"

"Oh, aye, just turn off that recording. Please."

The sound of weapon's fire and screaming died.

George slumped on to a stool, grabbed his specs from their perch on his nose and rubbed them with muddy fingers, smearing dirt all over them.

Raman Murti, Minister of Employment and Social

Security, was saying his prayers to the great god Vishnu when the message came blaring through. He clambered up from his knees and stared at the altar. It would appear that his prayers had not been answered.

Jennifer Alexander smiled blandly at the holo-cam, as they did standard lighting and colour checks.

"Read a few lines of the lead, so we can get a voice level."

She concentrated on the teleprompter embedded in her desk. "The mysterious interplanetary communications blackout continues into its second day."

She pushed away from the console. "Who wrote this junk, 'mysterious communications blackout continues'? My tongue's sure to trip on that!"

"Do I need to remind you?" the producer, Chris Charmin, snapped. "You did."

"Well, it's junk." She opened the drawer to reveal a keyboard and deleted the word "mysterious".

"What's the matter with you lately?" said Charmin. "You seem to be on edge."

The computer beeped, signalling an incoming message on the BAND worldwide syndicate line. Jennifer happily ignored his question as she bent over to read it.

Meanwhile the laser printer blazed with light. Charmin started. They hadn't seen a hard-copy confirmation of a news report since the Galactic War.

A single sheet was ejected on to a tray.

Charmin seized it. "Oh, goody! Maybe this is something interesting."

At her desk, the pigment drained from Jennifer Alexander's face as she read the communique.

FROM: NEWSNET INTERNATIONAL

DISTRIBUTION: UNIVERSAL

DATELINE: CENTRAL COMMAND, ALPS ARCHIPELAGOES — 3/9/ 2334

SUBJECT: WAR

AT TWELVE-HUNDRED HOURS, THE MARTIAN AUTHORITIES FIRED UPON COMMERCIAL CARRIER NIMROD EN ROUTE TO MARS. THIS OVERT ACT OF WAR TOOK PLACE IN NEUTRAL SPACE. FACED WITH SUCH HOSTILITIES, THE EARTH HAS NO OTHER CHOICE THAN TO DECLARE WAR ON ITS FORMER COLONIES . . .

5/9/2334

Nineteen-hundred Hours

The laundry inside a small closet on Level 2 seemed to acquire a life of its own. Had anybody been around to observe it, they would have seen a pile shift and stir, then rise as if growing and expanding.

An arm erupted from the folds of cloth, and a pincer hand yanked a jumpsuit from the top of the heap and tossed it aside. Then the metal arm swept impatiently across the top of the cabinet, knocking the laundry to the floor.

The robot wheeled. The photoreceptor lenses glinted as it spun, catching the minimal light and reflecting it again.

After three days, Robbie decided, it should be safe. The robot glided forward. The portal slid into the wall. The servo-mech plucked one of the photo-receptor cells from its socket and thrust it into the hall, using it like a periscope.

Non-uniformed Lilliputian clones lounged, scattered here, there and everywhere, but they took no notice of a housekeeping droid peeking from the laundry collection point. Robbie reseated its eye and slipped from the room. The robot meandered down the hall at a leisurely pace. The passengers looked bored, their faces downcast. A few stirred themselves to glower at the robot as it creaked past.

Robbie needed to locate the nearest maintenance cupboard. They were set up for just such contingencies as remedial repairs that a droid could make upon itself. They dotted the corridors of the ship, every eighteen metres.

The servo-mech noted the crossed-hammer repair label and headed straight for it. With a soft expiration, Robbie settled before the cabinet and pressed a button and a panel retracted into the wall. The robot selected the appropriate nozzle for the type of oil it needed and squirted the lubricant on the wheel as two apathetic passengers watched.

Then Robbie tested itself, rolling backward and forward.

Silence.

It replaced the nozzle and rolled away. Robbie retrieved a map of the vessel from AWS's memory banks, trying to find the easiest way back to the unoccupied portion of the ship.

By this time the robot had reached the end of the corridor where it emptied into a large chamber that spanned all four LQ levels. This area, Robbie noted on the map, had been apportioned off as the lounge.

With this many passengers, the room would be crowded at any time of day. Close to the dinner hour, it would be packed.

Robbie was going the wrong way. The robot braked and prepared to do a swift about-face, when its flight was arrested by the sight of the plasti-glas window that stretched from ceiling to floor.

The droid was riveted to the spot. Robbie had spent its entire tenure inside the enclosed environment of the Pennines Bathosphere – first with the Warren household and later, when Jennifer married, inside the Alexanders' home. The robot had never seen the sky much less the sun, moon and stars. It had no notion of space, nor the immensity of it.

Again Robbie did a rapid search of AWS's memory banks, drawing the pertinent files from its archives. Astronomy. The available data was huge, almost as immense as the universe itself.

Spellbound by the sight, the servo-mech was oblivious to the clones around it. Robbie crept toward the window, slowly, inexorably, as if drawn upon a string.

Click!

Robbie's photo lens touched the plasti-glas. The robot bounced back, coming to a rest. There it sat, shivering, as it quietly reordered its concept of its existence in relation to the known universe.

Allele Sigma Oogocyte placed his glass on the table, stuffed his hands in his pockets and contemplated the view. Mars had swelled from a red pinprick of light to a coin-sized disc. He made a rude noise.

Oogocyte, known as Og for short, was sorry now that he had opted for the Martian resettlement plan rather than deep space exploration. He'd had enough of feeling unwelcome, and he wondered if it was too late to change his mind.

His gaze flicked to his drink on the table. He grabbed the tumbler and stared at the table, with its funny ruffled skirt. Then he put his drink down and returned to his contemplation of the stars.

Og could talk to one of the captains – Zed, Zygote or Cyte. He snorted. He and how many other people? He couldn't be the only one who must be having second thoughts about Mars.

The disc radiated dully, almost belligerently, down at him. He winced and took a desultory kick at the table, but his foot met only air. He overbalanced, whirling and falling flat.

Og blushed, raised himself up on his elbow and

looked around the room. His drink and the table upon which it sat were nowhere to be seen.

Robbie felt the icy chill of the glass. The servo-mech scuttled away, not ready to be drafted into work or risk premature discovery. Its examination of the heavens would have to wait.

Robbie swooshed through the growing throng.

"We can't just change our minds," said one young Epsilon female. "They're hard pressed to feed us now. The provisions will never last until Alpha Centauri."

"The way I understand it, this ship could make the voyage all in one giant leap — in theory at least. The captains're just playing it safe by staging the journey in a series of graduated jumps because it's never been tested," argued her Tau opponent.

"So you mean the captains should risk the lives of some thousand crew members to take five thousand unwanted hitchhikers with them. Not to mention that they would be risking our lives too."

The male turned upon the Epsilon female and stabbed a finger at her. "Do you want to live constantly at war? Constantly with your guard up on a planet that doesn't want you?" The speaker slammed his glass down on what he thought was a table, as it darted away with a flicker of floral skirts.

The drink hung poised on the edge of the box for a second and went crashing to the floor.

Metal grated upon metal. The locking mechanism reeled right, then left and then right again. The hatch swung slowly outward. A disembodied hand appeared in the opening – a human hand – and stopped as the first words of a conversation penetrated to its as yet unseen possessor.

"What are we looking for?"

The hand snapped back into the wall.

"Early fruits."

"Won't the droids have harvested them already? I thought there were probes to indicate what level of ripeness, and—"

"Yes. Well, we're looking for anything they might have missed."

"Hmmph!" It seemed a fool's errand. "I'm not sure I'd recognize a ripe tomato unless there was a salad around it."

Just inside the hatch, a wary Dirk plastered himself against the wall. Circumstances seemed to be conspiring against him. First there'd been no leap, then his den had been unearthed – he assumed by a droid – then, the search, and now this.

He'd only just escaped search and seizure, thanks to that squeaky droid, probably the same one he'd heard his first day aboard ship. Possibly the same one that had got into the habit of dusting his room every day. Only a droid would be so obsessive as to trim string down to uniform-sized ends and loops.

The youth chortled. That droid had more than a squeaky wheel or two.

Dirk had come to the hydroponic unit for the first time, hoping to supplement his supply of dried food with something fresh. At one time he wouldn't have thought he'd ever get tired of rehydrated pizza, but he had with surprising rapidity. Four days was more than enough.

Because of the delay, Dirk's meagre rations would not stretch long enough, even to reach Mars. The same problem was evidently confronting the Lilliputian clones.

The youth knew from working with his father that the hydroponics farm was basically a mechanized domain, although human overseers were supposed to inspect the main systems of water and chemical feed daily, but not, usually, at this time. It should have been done earlier.

Even here the lazy foreman tended to rely on robots and droids, but now the industrious clones were harvesting by hand – something unheard of, in Dirk's experience.

He sagged against the hatch. What was going on? The passengers should have been long gone. Dirk cursed his size. His questions could be resolved easily, with less than five minutes spent in the lounge eavesdropping, if he didn't stick out like a sore thumb, literally standing head-and-shoulders above the rest.

Skulking in corners and hiding in tube-shafts, he could only glean things in pieces. From those pieces he had put together Dirk gathered that the Martians had been less than receptive to the grant of Martian land to the Lilliputs. Hence, the *Revenant* had slowed her pace to almost nothing.

But there was something else there too. Some undercurrent that he couldn't quite fathom.

His ears pricked and he leaned forward to listen.

"I think we can simplify this process. I'll ask the computer to pinpoint those fruits that are closest to ripeness and then instruct the droids to pick them. We can then attend to the vats."

"Great." The other sounded disgusted.

"I sure hope everyone likes veal."

"Only after it's cooked."

"If you're squeamish about such things, how'd you end up in hydroponics?"

"Just lucky, I guess." Responding to some unheard query, the man hurried on to continue, "I wasn't part of the original crew on either ship, and my position as technician was already filled. They put me here by default, probably because I have the expertise to repair the plumbing should it need it."

There was a swish and Dirk's ears popped with the slight change in pressure as the clones moved from one sealed chamber to another.

Still he waited until he heard the whir of drones moving up and down the aisle. He smiled. The Lilliputian clones had simplified the process for him too. He would just stay put until the drones had finished gathering the produce and then abscond with what he needed from their baskets.

Screwing up his courage, Dirk poked his head through the hatch and rammed into a semi-ripe pineapple.

"Ow!" He rubbed his nose and then tore the fruit from the stem. Dirk squirmed through the hole, circumventing the spiky leaves.

An alarm sounded somewhere, and a placidly harvesting droid dropped what it was doing and hastened over to the plant. Dirk had to jump aside to avoid collision with the drone.

It fussed over both the plant and stem, trying vainly to replace the fruit on the stalk. Dirk helped himself to the plums in the droid's basket.

The door to the meat vats opened, and a clone strode through and over to the computer console. Dirk did a nose dive between the rows.

The alarm died with a burble and a burp. The droid stopped trying to restore the fruit to the plant and pivoted, nearly running over Dirk as it returned to its appointed task. Dirk rolled to get out of the way, scratching his back on the pineapple's spined leaves.

Clambering on to his hands and knees, the youth peeked over the verdant points. The clone observed the work for a parsec and then returned to the meat production unit. Dirk scrambled back through the hatch and up the maintenance shaft.

He had a few plums. That would have to do.

Their regularly scheduled rest period did not find Ylon and Blast asleep inside their quarters. Instead, they conferred about the search. With so many passengers, it was one of the few times of the day they had to themselves.

Ylon pushed away on the table, balancing his chair on two legs, and rocked back and forth. "The captain's losing interest."

Blast sighed. "That's understandable, considering the circumstances. You can't blame Zed."

"But Dirk's here, I know it." Ylon thumped his chest. "I feel it. I knew he wouldn't let us go without saying goodbye. I just knew it."

Blast looked uncomfortably away.

The comm-unit trilled shrilly.

"Incoming call from Maisy Moor, of Pennines' Security."

Their eyes locked.

Ylon stood. "Now what?"

A dark face, striped with streaks of light and static caused by particles hitting the satellite dish, peered back at them.

"Maisy Moor here. Sorry to bother you during your

rest period, but we seem to have another little problem. One that perhaps you can help with."

"Yes?" Ylon said guardedly.

"I understand that you have been in contact with
Director Alexander regarding the disappearance of
the head of DSHQ. Did he, perchance, mention that
the human female Gwendolyn Finn is also missing?"

"Her too?" Blast said. "For how long?"

"A few days. It appears about the same time that
young Dirk went missing. We must assume that they
are together."

Blast was on her feet shouting. "And you're just
reporting it now?"

"We have first tried to search the facility. There
were indicators that the youth, at least, was still here.
The girl's father hoped she had gone back to the
orbital, but that search proved fruitless also. Now we
need you to broaden your investigation to include the
girl. Any luck so far finding the boy?"

The clones stiffened. "No, we have had other
priorities besides the hunt," said Ylon.

"As have we all. Well, this is Moor, Director of
Internal Affairs, signing out."

"Wonderful." sighed Ylon. "What else can go
wrong?"

Blast placed her finger to her lips. "Don't tempt
fate."

As if to confirm their suspicions, the communications

panel trilled a second time, signalling an in-house call.

"Lieutenants, Zed here. I'm afraid we're going to have to abandon the search. We have other priorities."

Ylon and Blast exchanged glances and nodded. The dayshift commander repeated Ylon's exact words.

"We're not going to ask you to stand down. You can do anything you want in your spare time, but we have moved from silent running to battle-ready status. According to intelligence the newly created Martian Navy is headed our way, with orders to confiscate this vessel or destroy it."

"Then we may continue the search during off hours?" ventured Blast.

"Yes, but I can't spare the crew."

"We'll get more volunteers from the passengers."

"Very good. You are to report immediately to cargo bay IV where sidearms are being issued." Blast's jaw dropped as she heard the order. "You'll be among the last to receive them."

Both snapped to attention and saluted. "Aye, aye, Captain!"

The visual dissolved.

As they hurried down the hall, Blast mused, "You know I think we've been going about this the wrong way. Why go scurrying all over the ship looking for them? Why don't we let them come to us?"

"Come to us? Are we going to issue an invitation, or what? If Dirk or Gwen were going to come to us don't you think they would have done it by now? It is obvious that their goal is to remain undercover until we have reached our destination, by which time it will be too late to send them back."

"Ah, but they're going to need supplies. Even if they brought some with them, they'll be in the same position as we are since we haven't made the leap to Mars, and they're going to need food eventually."

Light glimmered in Ylon's eyes as he grasped her idea. "All we have to do is stake out the kitchens."

"And the hydroponic farms."

Ylon considered this and inclined his head in assent. "Let's do it as soon as we've finished this."

The Martian fleet gathered. Gordon Rhys stormed around the bridge of his own little runabout, as the report came in about the *Nimrod*. His face was suffused with blood and his rage was such that he stammered as he spoke.

"Wha-wha-what could have possessed you? The plan was that we would present a united front against the *Revenant*, not go flying off in a lot of different directions, attacking vessels indiscriminately," Rhys said to the ship captain responsible.

"We are at war," the captain said mildly.

"We are now!" Rhys shouted. "Thanks to you, Earth has finally declared her military intentions."

The denounced captain looked bored. "War was inevitable. Besides, there were no orders to the contrary."

"Don't you understand? You should have commandeered the vessel. Even an unarmed freighter is of more value to us intact and whole than as space dust."

His rebuke fell on deaf ears.

"I don't think", challenged the other, "you have the stomach for war, and perhaps we should reconsider your appointment as leader."

Aft of the ship, Gwen simulated Dirk's actions inadvertently as she cowered inside a wall panel to the hollow bulkhead.

This was madness. She'd been stuck here for two days now. The place was crawling with clones. She was glad that she hadn't taken the easier option and commandeered a storage bay. If she hadn't been caught during the search, she most certainly would've been caught now.

The search had not surprised her. In fact, she had been expecting it and touched that her father had noticed her missing so soon, but now the Lilliputian clones were breaking into cargo bay IV, a storage area clearly designated for use after they had arrived at their destination.

If she didn't move quickly, she really would be

trapped inside this bulkhead. She rose, her curiosity piqued.

What were they doing?

Gwen gouged at a panel; it snapped off in her hands to create an exit into the adjoining bay.

She concentrated, trying to pinpoint the Lilliputs' exact location from her den.

The voices were muffled. One or two bays away. She crawled through the opening and ambled to the entrance. She peeped around the corner and saw activity some three doors down.

The weapons stores.

Gwen withdrew into the room. *What did they need weapons for?*

Again, she risked a peek. A table had been set up and a queue had formed.

The clone behind the table bellowed a name. "Mitochondrial Gamma?"

A uniformed officer approached the table. Someone handed him a weapon. He strapped it into place and moved away.

"Morula Alpha."

Another officer advanced to retrieve her weapon.

"Oogocyte ..."

The girl's face blanched, for there bringing up the rear were Ylon and Blast. With twenty-six basic somatypes and only limited variations within the somatypes, it was a little hard to tell the clones apart sometimes, but Gwen had known her Lilliputian friends long enough to recognize them by their mannerisms if nothing else.

Gwen recoiled into her cargo bay to rest her cheek against the cool metal and tried to think.

Sidearms. Sidearms were weapons designed for close combat. Why sidearms?

Gwen glanced around her. What was stored in this adjacent bay? Would they come here next?

This was a good time, she decided, to exit stage left. She pressed her spine flat against the wall, as if, by following its contours, she could make herself invisible. She heeded this same philosophy as she slunk around the door, back against the wall, and it stood her in good stead, for she cast no shadow as she continued up the hall. Dressed as she was in dull-grey jumpsuit, Gwen appeared little more than a ripple in the paintwork. She had only gone a few metres when she froze.

A muscle in her face twitched as her mind made the connection. She'd lived long enough in the military to recognize that the only need for sidearms was in case of conflict, and this meant war.

7/9/2334

Fourteen-hundred Hours

Maisy Moor's Lilliputian assistant stalked through the door with a high prancing step, snapped to attention and saluted the Director of Internal Affairs. Ms Moor smiled inwardly. She liked the Lilliputians. She admired their precision and their discipline, and she often wished full-grown humans were more like their cloned progeny.

Her assistant, an exuberant Theta model, held his arm stiff, until Moor had acknowledged his salute with one of her own. He relaxed and propped himself casually against her desk.

"How is it out there?" she asked.

"You wouldn't believe it," he said with a rush of air.

Her eyebrow twitched. "There are more?" The

director groaned. "Why don't they go home? Don't they realize we have no ships? No army or navy? No need for recruits?"

The clone looked troubled. "But you do have ships."

"Not of, ah, er, human-size. Not armed and ready for battle."

"So?" He waved an arm expansively. "I don't understand. We were bred for war. Why don't you use the resources available? Why don't you use us?"

"Since the original conflict evolved over our right to grant land, and since the Lilliputians' right to possess that land has been called into doubt, and since the final resolution includes your people settling on Mars, the council believe it would be counterproductive to send the clones as assault troops. This would only increase Martian hostility towards your people and impede plans for eventual resettlement."

Lieutenant Theta whistled. "That is a far-sighted view."

The director chuckled humourlessly. "Yes, I know it's not a very human characteristic, but every once in a while we can surprise you. Besides, I believe and I think the council agree, it's about time we started fighting our own battles, even if it means the war has to be put off until we've been able to arm a few ships."

"Well," said Theta returning to the topic at hand,

"wanted or not, the volunteers outside are getting restive. Perhaps you should speak to them."

"I wouldn't know what to say."

He regarded her expectantly.

The security director exhaled. "All right. Let's see what we can do."

Maisy Moor moved around her desk and into the front office, which was, due to its high visibility, situated near the central park dome. She gaped at the queue. It seemed to stretch for miles, although she knew this could not be true. The entire Pennines Bathosphere was only twenty-one miles in diameter. The associated hydroponics farms and storage facilities covered another eighteen miles of ocean floor. The queue only wrapped its way around the park dome twice.

She deflated. "Good grief! I thought after a while they'd get bored and go away."

"There is", commented Theta, "a lot more fighting spirit in the human species than one might anticipate."

Maisy winced. "Yes, witness three hundred years of war."

"Will you speak to them?"

"What do you recommend I say? I've told them already that we aren't looking for volunteers – that recruitment, when it becomes necessary, will be announced. I've tried threats, from loss of employment to arrest, and you can see the result."

The clone weighed her question seriously. "You could, I suppose, let them sign up."

"Sign up for what?"

"For whatever. Take their names and residential codes and tell them that they will be one of the first contacted when the time comes."

"What time?"

"Who knows? Who even cares? But it would get the line moving and pacify tempers that are becoming a bit frayed with all the standing about. Most importantly, it would get them off the streets and back to their places of employment where they belong."

"Of course, Theta. You're a genius." Maisy Moor had to resist the impulse to sweep the clone off his feet, as one would a child. It would show a lack of respect for someone who, despite his size, was an adult, and she could imagine that from a Lilliputian point of view it would be quite disconcerting.

"Set up tables in front of the facility right away, and drag everyone away from their normal duties. I want to be able to seat at least twenty people at a time. Perhaps they'll calm down when they see they can sit down."

Twenty minutes later, the secretarial staff had gathered. Maisy noted their confusion at being pulled from their routine activities and wondered if she had made the right decision. She had elected the less adaptable adult humans to greet the "volunteers" rather than the Lilliputs since the clones seemed to have an inflammatory effect on the populace.

This was, Moor surmised, in direct measure to humanity's debt to the clones.

Armed Lilliputian guards would flank the table while the remainder of the troop would patrol the park where they could be used to much better effect in crowd control.

Director Moor paced to and fro, giving last-minute instructions.

"You will take only their names, residential codes and vid-phone connections," Moor faltered, "and their social security numbers. That will make this seem more official. If there are any enquiries, just say they will be among the first contacted. Remember, keep it brief. The point is to get the line moving and persuade them to leave."

"But I thought we weren't doing any active recruiting."

"We aren't, but we will eventually if things don't work out, and we might as well have a list of those people who are eager to join the fight."

Jennifer Alexander confronted the spectacle in the dome with mixed emotions. Not since the previous food crisis – before they had reinstituted the old system of guaranteed employment – had she seen this kind of crowd. But this group was orderly, lined up in neat little queues, as if they were waiting for some long, non-existent bus, or a Space Thugs concert.

No, Jennifer admonished herself, people waiting for a concert wouldn't be nearly so tractable.

She fiddled with her gear, glad that Charmin had released her from her desk to do this man-on-the-street poll, for the only thing Jennifer did while she was in the office was worry about Dirk.

Six days had passed and still no word. She was frantic. Her son was out there somewhere in space – he had to be, a search of the facility had yielded nothing – and, even if it was slow getting started, there was a war going on. Worse, he had hitched a ride on the same vehicle that the Martians had sworn to capture or annihilate.

Jennifer forced her mind back to her work and scanned the dome. All she had to do was find the nearest security-cam link-up to AWS. With this many people, getting an interview would be a snap.

She spied the nearest camera and moved into position. "Hello, sir, I'm—"

"Hey! You're Jennifer Alexander, the presenter."

"That's right."

"Am I gonna get interviewed?"

"You are being interviewed."

"Really? Am I on camera?"

"Yes, you are."

"Hi, Mom!" He waved into empty space.

Jennifer grinned. Some things never changed.

There was always one. She'd have to edit the salutation from the footage. "Sir, may I ask what are you doing here?"

His chest expanded and he leered at her. "I'm signing up. There's a war on, you know. Of course you know. I heard it from you." He elbowed his companion. "I'm gonna go get me some Martians."

"You mean you want to fight?"

"Yeah, I'm ready for a fight. I'm tired of being trapped in a goldfish bowl. The way I figure it, you can't get off this planet any other way unless you're a soldier, or a clone." He glowered at the nearest security officer strolling through the throng.

"Don't you think the government should pursue diplomatic channels first?" she asked.

"Why? They're Terran subjects. They're subject to Terran laws, just like everybody else."

"It could be argued that many of the inhabitants have been on Mars for generations and therefore are no longer Terran."

"Well, they're from here originally, even if they moved to Mars from the Moon. All people emigrated from here, and we can't have Earth's subjects declaring their independence left, right and centre, or we're gonna have anarchy."

He settled back and concluded his argument, fully convinced of its validity. "Who knows, I may wanna settle on Mars someday. Do I want to let a bunch of dumb Martians keep me out?"

His companion chimed in. "Give 'em a good trouncing. Let them know we haven't gone soft here on Earth."

Jennifer tried a different tactic. "What about sending the Lilliputian clones in? I mean, that is the function for which they were designed."

"Clones? No, sir!" said the first man. "This is *our* fight. Big people against big people. Leave 'em outa it. I mean you can't really trust 'em, can you?"

"Actually, you can," interjected the next gentleman in line. "The clones, bred for the military, are a lot more trustworthy than your average human."

Jennifer turned to him. He seemed a lot more rational than the first two. "That's an unusual perspective. Who are you, sir?"

"I'm a psychologist and I've seen their personality profiles. Much more stable than the human, the clone is. Much more."

"If you're a psychologist, why have you come down to enlist?"

"I suppose for pretty much the same reason everyone else has. Patriotism. Unity of purpose. The three planets must stand together or fall apart. Quite literally."

"War is hardly unifying."

"Have you ever seen a group this large assembled without incident? Many of these people have been here for two days, yet they are calmly waiting their turn. Yes, I'd say war is unifying, in a way."

She looked incredulous.

He noticed her perplexed expression and explained. "As far as I'm concerned, they never should've stopped the war. Man is a predatory animal, a competitive animal. Historically speaking, there's always been war and there probably always will be."

The others listening to his conversation agreed. "I'll say! Things were a lot better during the Conflict and they've only just started getting better since we've reverted to the old war-time structure. War is just the shot in the arm man needs."

His companion pounded his chest. "Let's blow those suckers from here to kingdom come."

Despite the climate-controlled environment in the bathosphere with its fixed temperature of 22 degrees centigrade, Jennifer Alexander felt chilled to the bone.

A few minutes later, Jennifer Alexander wriggled from her blazer and flopped into her chair.

"Have you heard?" Charmin came prancing into the room, grinning. "We've won our first battle."

She gawped at the man. He bent over her console and typed in the Newsnet Band, with a release directly from Central HQ in the Alps. She read:

... EARTH HAS MET THE FIRST CONFRONTATION OF THE WAR AND EMERGED VICTORIOUS WHEN MARTIAN AGENTS WERE APPRE-HENDED, WITHOUT BLOODSHED, AS THEY ENTERED THE PENNINES COMPOUND...

"But—" She had heard about the incident from her husband. Two nights previous, a hapless merchant, whose radio had gone on the fritz, and his crew had been arrested on arrival at the port facility. The men had submitted without so much as a murmur, blithely unaware of the war.

"This is ridiculous!" She slapped the terminal.

"I know. Read on," he said.

THE HEAVILY ARMED SHIP WAS COMMANDEERED AS PART OF AN OVERALL STRATEGY . . .

"All Martian ships are armoured," she grumbled, "It's not like he came with guns blazing to take on the entire Earth forces."

"Yes, isn't war wonderful?" Charmin tap-danced gaily around the room. "It's back to business as usual. No more lost cats and dogs stories. Or grandmothers suffering from gout for the first time in centuries due to the sporadic food supply. News. Real news."

"A pack of lies," she shouted.

"This is war," he said.

Jennifer Alexander slumped deeper into her chair. "Right!"

The holographic image of Francis Willard, head of central committee, seemed to fill the entire conference room of DSHQ.

"We have called this, our first war tribunal, as a means of devising strategy. Are all the council members present and accounted for?" He peered into

114

the camera, giving the impression that he was staring directly into George's eyes.

Alexander slouched, a sign of his contempt for the whole proceedings.

"Our declaration has caught us unprepared. We humans", he lingered over the word, "are a peaceful people, and we have not actually fought in a war for centuries."

Dirk's father nearly choked on his laughter. He put his hand over his mouth and began to cough.

"The reality of our situation is bleak," said Willard. "We have no armed ships able to house a full-sized human crew. No armada with which we can fight a battle much less a war."

"But the seizures—" commented Barrymore-Smythe.

"So far, we've only been able to appropriate three Martian vessels, two of which are docked on the Moon. Since we have yet to ascertain where Lunar sympathies lie, we have no idea what will become of those ships. The Lunar authorities have been ordered to release them to Earth, but have yet to comply. We cannot guarantee the vessels will be forthcoming.

"According to our orbital refit stations, and I'm sure the head of DSHQ would confirm this if he were present," Willard glowered at the coughing George, "it would take years to build a single squadron from scratch, and months were we to try to fit peacetime crafts, such as cargo carriers and passenger ships, with new weapons."

He stopped and spread his arms wide in a gesture of frustration. "All our technology and our weaponry have gone into the Lilliputian fleet, and we agree that we should not rely upon the little people, particularly if we wish to use Mars for their eventual relocation. No need to increase animosity between the two races."

George started. Perhaps there was hope for Earth yet. The next sentence crushed that hope.

"Therefore," said Willard, "we have no other choice, but to dismantle the Lilliputian fleet and adapt those weapons to our needs."

And George was on his feet, shouting, "What? You can't mean that!"

The director cast Dirk's father an oblique stare. "I gather we have one dissenting vote."

Willard faced Alexander, staddle-footed, arms akimbo. "You of all people should wish to see this policy adopted. Think of your son."

George subsided and sat. "I *am* thinking of my son. If we dismantle the Lilliputian fleet, we will be left defenceless. The danger is real, and the danger is *now*. The *Revenant* can't wait even a month while we cannibalize war vessels in hopes of creating a human-sized fleet."

"The *Revenant* is the biggest, fastest, most highly

advanced ship ever built," said Willard. "The crew'll have to fend for themselves."

George looked up. "But—"

"Or perhaps we should send our one armoured vehicle, the recently appropriated Martian craft." He glanced behind him. "Is the radio is fixed?" Willard returned his attention to his audience. "We can man it with a human crew. It will provide a show of support."

Willard clapped his hands. "We must vote. The secretary will read you the proposal."

The secretary repeated the main points. "Whereas Earth finds itself in a state of war with another human population. Given also that we have agreed that in this contest, human must fight human. All those in favour of dismantling the old *Galactic War* fleet", he emphasized the words, "to create an armada capable of handling human crew, type in your vote." The secretary waited a minute or two.

"Those who oppose?"

George slammed his hand on the no button and waited as the votes were cast and tallied.

Dirk's father was somewhat appeased to see that, this time, the vote was not unanimous. Many did not agree with Central's policy of destroying the only armada Earth had.

He drummed his fingers against the tabletop irritably. The only salvation George could see for the *Revenant* – and for his son – was if the Lilliputs went to their rescue. Yet this be would doing the very same thing that they had so far abstained from doing – using the warrior clones to fight their battles.

Strictly, George assured himself, as a defensive measure. He chewed on his lip. The proposal squeaked through by the narrowest of margins.

Fools! The verdict was in, and there wasn't much he could do about it.

"We must agree to set a date for a formal meeting of parliament to set policy..."

Various dates were discussed. George fumed, took off his specs and polished them furiously. The meeting broke up.

Back rigid, he rose and shouldered his way through the milling members. He pounded down the hall to the lift. The DSHQ staff gave him a wide berth, for his countenance was dark as a thunderous sky.

The lift door whooshed open and a smile slid across George's face, to be instantly suppressed.

Unless, of course, he found some way to prevent the implementation of their plan...

Perry Finn wandered into his one-time offices to check his mail. His arms were full when the security chief Wilbur Gottwald appeared at the door.

"A priority one message for you, sir," he said.

Finn dropped the packages and sat at the communications console. Gottwald ducked from the room to give his superior privacy.

The dot matrix on the screen sparkled, darting thither and yon as static danced across the screen. The image solidified. George Alexander's frowning face peered out at Finn.

Dirk's father didn't waste time on niceties.

"Are you alone?" he said.

Finn scowled and simply nodded in the affirmative. "For now."

"Good. We have a secure line. You will shortly be receiving orders from Central. I, uh, er, want you to ignore them."

Finn's eyes narrowed and he wondered if this were some kind of test of his loyalty. "Just what do you have in mind?"

"The central parliament has just passed a proposal to dismantle the entire Lilliputian fleet, using those parts and weapons needed to arm freighters and passenger vessels to create a human armada." Alexander lowered his voice and canted forward conspiratorially. "You realize we cannot let them do this. The Lilliputian fleet is the only hope we have to see our children alive again."

Finn started. "Don't they realize if they disassemble the only fleet we have, it will leave Earth defenceless until new ships have been constructed or the old ones modified?"

"Yes, I mentioned that, but Central doesn't seem to care. For now the resolution stands and the die is cast. The orders for the refit should be coming through any minute now. Can you see that they get lost for a while?"

"Lost? I don't know about lost." Finn mused over the problem that had been presented to him.

"I'm going to round up the Lilliputian leaders and organize transport. That will be something of a challenge," said George, more to himself than to Finn. "Will you see that they get to their ships, if I get them, and manage to get them off world? I know it's a tall order."

"Might I suggest that the best way to confront this problem is directly. We have no time to dissemble."

"I'm not sure I understand."

"The Lilliputian fleet is small."

"Of course it's small!" George snapped. "What would you expect?"

Finn went on smoothly. "So small, in fact, that it's difficult for human repair crew to work in the ships. Speed in this situation is essential. What would be more natural than to import people of the, ah, appropriate size to do this work?"

"Ah," said George as the light of realization dawned in his eyes.

"Are they willing to fight to defend Earth?"

"Yes, I'm sure of it. They're more than willing now and do not really understand why we haven't sent them off yet."

Finn nodded tersely. "I'll see what I can do."

Just then Gwen's father heard an abortive cry,

quickly strangled as Gottwald came stumbling into the room, his face as white as a sheet.

"I don't believe it." The security chief sagged against the edge of the console. "They want us to dismember the fleet."

"It would appear that your message has got through." Finn said to George. "This is Finn, signing off." He thumbed a toggle and turned to the youth. "You are surprised?"

"Aren't you?"

Finn sniffed. The kid was still young and couldn't quite fathom the insanities of man.

"We have additional orders straight from DSHQ. We are to bring the Lilliputian crews up."

"Pardon? I mean, won't they object to their ships being disassembled?"

"The vessels are too small to accommodate your average worker. Removing single weapons is exacting work that needs to be done by hand. The Lilliputs know their ships. They will dismantle them if they don't want to see them destroyed in the process, I'm sure. See that these additional orders are circulated among all the orbital stations."

"Shouldn't DSHQ do this?"

"I'm sure they have. This is just to make sure that the word gets around. Things are pretty hectic groundside."

The young lieutenant scratched his head. "Sure doesn't make sense to tear apart the only armada we have. How do they know they can adapt the weaponry to larger ships?"

"Ours is not to reason why," Finn commented wryly.

"Oh yes," said Gottwald. "We've been stripped of our security personnel."

"You're kidding?"

"They plan to send a human escort to accompany the *Revenant* to Mars, and they want former military personnel to staff her. It would seem that most of them reside here, as part of our security system."

Finn smirked. He would not mind seeing the last of Marks's hand-picked security organization.

"Good riddance!" Finn mumbled.

"That leaves us a little short of staff."

"That's all right. I'm sure you can manage. We have qualified personnel right here."

Finn extended his hand and took the orders from the bemused Gottwald. "I'll see that the station commander Morgan gets this."

Ten faces glowered down at Gordon Rhys as the entire wall of his bridge was given over to an emergency meeting of the war council – a meeting not called by himself. Gordon pursed his lips. Not a good sign. No matter how hard he tried to hold them back, events were rapidly spiralling out of his control.

Rhys sat in the captain's chair, his features carefully schooled into an expression of neutrality. He found the mantle of leadership an ill-fitting garment. Already, he'd had had more than enough trouble with the fractious officers of the hastily-concocted Martian fleet.

The first officer towered over Rhys, standing one step behind in what should have been a position of deference or respect. Why, then, did Rhys feel threatened? He had to repress the urge to cast a surreptitious glance over his shoulder at the man, as the leader tried to call the more unruly captains back into line.

"The *Nimrod* was unnecessary, and I tell you that we are not going to have a repeat performance. We are not going to destroy the *Revenant*. We're going to capture her."

"You don't seem to grasp that this is a war!"

"Ah, but I do, and the *Revenant* is much too valuable a piece of equipment to our side to destroy her."

"You don't even seem to grasp the basic concept of war, do you?"

"If that concept includes useless and wanton destruction, then that is true."

As a group, the committee members frowned. One nodded at the first officer, and Rhys felt a cold cylinder of pressure on the back of his skull, just below the ear.

The commander recognized it immediately as the muzzle of a gun. His eyes rolled wildly in his sockets, but he did not move, nor turn to see whether it was a lethal laser or the milder stun gun.

"You are being relieved of your command."

"You elected me!" Rhys said indignantly, with as much bravado as he could muster.

"And we can replace you if we choose. Your attitude has been obstreperous and obstructive. One wonders which side you are on."

"And who will my replacement be?" Rhys spat. "You?"

"That is none of your concern. You will be escorted to your quarters and held there until we decide if you should be tried for treason."

Former nightshift captain of the *Thanatos* Morula Zed fidgeted restlessly in the queue. DSHQ had commanded the clones to assist with the dismantling of the ships in Dirk's name, and no one on Earth or her orbitals had thought to question the source.

Their transport had accomplished two goals, getting the crews to their ships and delaying disassembly until the "hands" to accomplish it were available.

The lucky ones had taken the more comfortable shuttle quite openly, but time was running out. Already the cumbersome machinery of government was lumbering into action. Theirs were the last few squads to be returned to their ships and they would have to be smuggled aboard, before the absence of the entire Lilliputian contingent was noticed.

Morula was one of the few among the *Thanatos*'s crew who had opted to stay with the fleet on Earth. She did not want to start a new life elsewhere or explore new worlds. She liked the old one, and if that meant policing the skies between Earth and the Moon, then so be it.

In honour of her years of service aboard the *Thanatos*, Morula had been given a ship of her own. She was dayshift captain for the first time in her life.

Council member Alexander met them at the dock, murmuring a few words of encouragement to each as they boarded, and Morula decided that she liked this human, who had been so overshadowed by his son.

Once inside the vessel, she planted herself next to the door, which had the only porthole in the entire ship, and refused to budge. She didn't mind being crammed on this freighter – she was used to tight places and she'd do almost anything to save her first real command – but Morula Zed wouldn't fly blind.

The tiny captain watched from her vantage point next to the door, noting that only the young Dirk's father attended them. George Alexander even refuelled the vessel with his own hands, ensuring there would be no records of this take-off and its unprecedented cargo noted anywhere, not even in the belly of some drone.

The man plucked his glasses from his nose and scrubbed them as the crew performed a preflight check. Then Alexander crammed the protective head-gear over his skull, pulled the ears flaps down and stepped back, hands in his pocket, as the lift took them to the launch pad.

He lowered the protective goggles to shield his face.

Morula settled against the wall, content now that they were on their way, and she grunted. She could not believe human obduracy. They dithered, immobilized by some curious sense of right and wrong, and left the *Revenant* to face the wrath of Mars alone. She might never understand this thing called human pride.

The Lilliputian clones had needed no urging to fight, even before they had heard about the human plans for their ships. They had always been ready for battle, but rather than lose their fleet, they would run; they would hide from their Terran masters, even if it meant mutiny.

And *they* would go the aid of their comrades since it would appear no one else was going to. A skeleton contingent of some two squadrons would stay behind to protect Earth. It would be more than enough to hold off anything but a concerted of attack of the entire Martian fleet. And no such assault could hope to succeed without the element of surprise, and that would be lost since the enemy armada must assuredly pass the Lilliputian fleet as they made their way to Mars.

They would all lift off at once. If they did, there was

nothing any human agency could do to stop them, except through AWS. Only the youthful Dirk knew enough about the software to recognize that the computer had the capacity to override theirs. And he had gone.

By the time someone thought of it many of their craft would be long gone, having shot-putted out into space using the station as a fulcrum. Others, however, would tarry and possibly be subject to computer recall, if anyone thought to do it.

Their group was the last. The others had been secreted aboard their respective vessels. They waited; they prepared.

They had spent their time since George Alexander had contacted them deciding who would catapult, who would not; when and in what direction. It was like co-ordinating an extremely complex, and potentially lethal, ballet. For the ships had to leave simultaneously, even those using standard propulsion engines. Thus the clones were working in not just three dimensions, but four. The momentum of their "shot" had to be timed just right or they might send the station spinning off into space or, worse, leave it stationary but spinning like a top and crushing everyone aboard her under the sudden flux in gravitational pull.

In addition, they could easily crash into one another within the cramped sphere of the orbital. Yet any attempt to leave singly or as a squadron, thereby permitting a less congested exit, would be suspicious from the Earth's point of view. The idea was to scatter rather than move *en masse*. They would take nearly as many routes to Mars as there would be ships, using anything that fell in their path as a catapult.

The way Morula figured it, if she pressed hard, if she squeezed every ounce of power from the engines, used every trick in the book from catapult to timed leap – or a combination of the two – with a bit of luck she could reach the *Revenant* in five days.

Those remaining would also scatter, using standard engines and acting as decoys to lead their Terran masters astray, leaving the humans to try and track Lilliputian progress and divine their purpose. She smiled. Let them think the clones had run away; it would be good for humanity to understand why they needed their smaller cousins.

It was a good plan as long as there were no mistakes in their arithmetic, no miscalculations on their part. If that were the case they'd end up scattered as salvage across the night sky, or buried somewhere beyond time under the starless blanket of ultra-space.

The orbital reeled under the advent of the little people as each arriving shuttle disgorged several companies of Lilliputian clones. The newly appointed station commander, Joyce Morgan, was stunned by the numbers. Surely there were too many?

As each new shuttle-load was assimilated into the

orbital, disappearing without a trace, she relaxed a bit. She had been wrong about the numbers.

Then another shipload would arrive and her incredulity rise even higher.

Morgan retreated to the safety of her office and mused. Surely they had more than enough clones for their purposes? She ambled over to the wall console and keyed in a shot of the station. She studied the orbital, so stark and white in contrast to the raven black of night.

Somewhere overhead, the Moon leered down on the arachnid structure, bleaching it even more until the bridges that spanned the gaps shone a blinding white. The station resembled a spider's web, with its web-like extensions stacked along a central axis.

At the end of each arm, a ship slumbered in a net cradle.

There was the muffled thud of contact as another ship docked. Morgan recoiled.

"Computer? What ship is this?"

"A Lunar freighter, registered with the Food Services Corp. Cargo manifest states it's carrying luxury foods."

"Luxury foods? Since when has Earth started exporting food?"

"According to my data, Earth doesn't export food. It's primarily an importer."

"Exactly." She gazed at the station. It revolved in

its eternal dance. "Have all the Lilliputian crews arrived?"

"Three have yet to log in," the computer replied.

"Where have the clones all gone?"

"Unknown. Many variables here." The voder voice sounded wounded. "One must presume they are somewhere aboard the station."

"It was a rhetorical question. As small as they are, there were too many of the Lilliputs to have just vanished. Where could they be?"

"Aboard their ships?"

She eyed the crafts sleeping in their beds. Her mouth dropped open and snapped shut.

"Of course! Order all the vessels searched."

"Searched? Looking for?"

"Clones, of course."

The computer hesitated a nanosecond and remarked serenely, "But of course. Isn't that where they're supposed to be?"

"Why has no work been started?"

"Excuse me," said AWS. "We have no security personnel. They were all – except the chief – drafted into the war effort."

"Then get me the chief of security."

Glancing nervously over his shoulder, Perry Finn escorted the three Lilliputian crews to their respective cruisers. The last commander, a Zed female, saluted him crisply. He responded instinctively, saluting himself, and then blushed. He let his hand drop. He was in the military no more.

"Where will you go?" he said.

"Where do you think?" Morula replied.

The implant in his ear trilled.

"Yes," Finn replied into the comm-unit. "I'm sorry, commander, I can't seem to hear you." He tugged at his ear lobe. "There must be something wrong with the implant. I'll be there in a moment."

"Problems?"

"We are found out. You must not linger. Get on your ships and go. Now!"

Morula Zed commanded the private to unclamp the vessel from the cradle as she hastened towards the bridge, giving orders as she went.

"Get the other ships on the horn!" she shouted. "Let's get this show on the road."

She stormed on to the bridge as her fellow commanders logged in one by one.

The screen sprang to life, with images of the captain and the bridge replicated a hundred times as all crews linked into a common channel.

Morula explained the urgency of their situation. The crew fanned out behind her. The CTO bent over the computer, performing delicate calculations while the helmsman ran standard checks.

"Are we ready?"

"Trajectory calculated and noted. Path logged in," said the CTO.

"Engines check out?"

"Ready."

From a hundred different screens, a hundred different faces, a hundred different voices said: "Go!"

The vessels uncoupled from their moorings at once, and the station rocked.

The pilot steered the craft away from the orbital. Some of the ships winked out. Others hovered, jockeying for position. Some accelerated, only to vanish in a streak of light. It was lunacy, and Morula was sure they were going to collide with another vessel.

She double-checked her harness, crossed her fingers and counted ... one ... two ... three ... four ... five ... until the program kicked in.

Morula Zed was pressed against her seat as they gathered speed. The tractor beam lashed out, latching on to the station, and the captain wondered whether this would be the time they would send the orbital pivoting off course.

Then it was too late to wonder or worry as they were catapulted away from the station into darkness. The timed-leap function took over and the smear of stars was replaced by pitch. Another white object, most likely a ship, went careering past, missing them by only a few scant metres.

They would stay in ultra-space until the computer

indicated they'd lost the forward impetus of their shot.

Morula gazed blearily at the screen, for leaps had a curiously disorienting effect on the mind and a gut-wrenching effect on the body. Motion was blurred, creating a series of flickering images. Normal movement was revealed by several figures superimposed over the other. If a person was, for example, lifting his arm, the observer saw many arms each with the position slightly altered, attached to a single, and stationary, shoulder. So a person walking appeared as succession of diaphanous doubles, like a badly synched holograph.

Morula gulped back nausea and wiped sweat from her brow. The heavens reappeared, empty and quiet.

The crew applauded. They'd survived the escape and emerged without materializing in another ship.

"Find the next object," Morula barked the order, "tanker, liner or civilian cargo carrier."

"Aye, aye, Captain!"

The nightshift captain tapped the arm of the chair. "I believe I'll go get some sleep."

The stress on the craft would be great, problems had been solved only on the Manta-style *Revenant*, not upon the smaller Dolphin cruiser. But what could provide a greater challenge to her skill than to see her ship through this unscathed?

"Cargo carrier on the port bow."

"Calculate the leap!"

"Done."

"Go!"

And the crew dissolved into a series of mysterious *doppelgängers* once more.

At the end of their work-shift Ylon and Blast hurried to relieve the volunteers who guarded the kitchens. The search had long since been abandoned. They spoke now in hushed tones, for to speak much above a whisper caused an echo effect in the huge hall.

Blast would occasionally peek over her shoulder to make sure they weren't being followed. She still hadn't got used to the immensity of the ship. Sometimes the clone wished that Refit had taken the trouble to lower the ceiling to Lilliputian height, even if it meant creating dead space.

No, she thought. That would only mean there were more places for Dirk and Gwen to hide.

Considering their current predicament, though, they could easily have halved the levels, dividing each floor in two, and doubling their space for housing passengers. Then the captain could have taken on more crew and perhaps accommodated those who wanted to continue to Alpha Centauri. As it was, horizontal, and not vertical, space was at a premium, and all that massive expanse above her head was wasted anyway. She drew her thoughts from the empty space overhead and concentrated on what her partner was saying.

"I just hope we're the ones that stumble across them, and not somebody else."

Of course, the couple would be treated with strict military protocol, by the book. Which, for Dirk, who was AWOL at a time of war, included immediate execution for treason, although neither clone could believe that it would go that far. Most likely they'd get the brig, assuming it wasn't already occupied by some of their unplanned guests.

She nodded her head in mute agreement. "The odds are in our favour that they will come to the kitchens in the evening after the final meal has been served. Recently crew have been present in the kitchens during the day, but not at night. Then it becomes the provenance of droids once more.

"Besides," she concluded, "it is the largest meal of the day, after all, and Dirk has a healthy appetite."

"If I know our friend Dirk, he planned ahead," said Ylon. "He brought stores along."

"The computer print-outs would appear to support that conclusion. Not enough food is missing to feed the two of them, although there have been some shortages, beyond those we might expect. Unfortunately, it appears to be just enough – in terms of caloric value – to feed one individual not two. Could we be wrong in assuming that they're both here?"

"They would crave variety. Perhaps they only planned to have their stores fill part of their needs. I don't know where they've hidden themselves, but I can't imagine they were able to bring enough food to last for the duration."

"And they would need fresh fruit to satisfy their requirements for vitamin C."

The clones slowed as they reached the end of the corridor.

"Which leads us to the next question, hydroponics or kitchens?" He pulled a single die from his pocket. "You choose."

"Six. The kitchens."

Ylon threw the die against the wall. It boomed against the metal bulkhead. Blast flinched.

"Maybe we need a less noisy way to choose," mumbled Ylon. He stared at the numbers. "Six! I swear, Blast, how do you do that?"

"Hope I'm right about the kitchens too," said Blast.

"Well, it *is* where most of the food has been disappearing."

"Not really, it's only where we have the most accurate records," advised Blast. She put her finger to her lips, and they stole forward, gliding soundlessly through the door where they split up, each heading for different areas of the room.

Blast slid along the wall as she made her way to replace one of their volunteers; Ylon would relieve the second. Their two guards were stationed on opposite sides of the room, next to the two main inlet and outlet vents that were large enough to accommodate a 1.8-metre-tall human.

She could see one of the guards now, hidden next to the grill.

She mouthed the word. "Anything?"

The Chi male wrinkled his nose and shrugged.

She nodded dismissal. He followed her circuitous path to the door. As soon as he and his partner had left, the illumination dwindled until only the light of the radiant floorboards remained.

Blast hunkered down to wait. After two nights on sentry duty without sleep, he fell into a light doze straight away.

Rhys had been listening to the sound of battle for days now. They weren't even fighting the right adversary, presuming that Earth was the avowed enemy. Instead, his compatriots were fighting among themselves to see who would fill the vacuum they had created when he had been deposed – like dogs over a bone. The very crisis his nomination had been meant to avert was upon them.

In the interim, he had received no news, no real food. Rhys threw the canned bread down in disgust. Speaking of dogs, this wasn't something he'd feed to his. For in this as in everything else, the Martians harkened back to the old ways, reintroducing species that man had not seen since the Flood. Some even talked about returning to a more humane form of farming and not relying upon cloned, vat-grown beef.

BOOM!

The ship bucked and rolled. *They were under attack!*

Rhys sprang to his feet and shook his fist at his unseen adversary. Perversely he hoped that they were fighting amongst themselves. He did not believe that Mars's disorganized fleet could survive a battle against the consolidated Earth's forces for more than a few hours. The more competent clones would have made short work of them.

He cursed himself. He should have kept his opinions, no matter how well advised, to himself. His was the only voice of reason and it could not be heard above the din of battle.

The entrance to his quarters chimed. He gaped at it. No one bothered with the formality of requesting admittance from a prisoner. Rhys winced. This visit must be "official".

The charge of treason hung like the sword of Damocles over his head.

"Who is it?"

"Your first, sir."

Sir? Rhys blinked. Last time the two had spoken, his first officer had not been quite so courtly. He had swaggered like a popinjay and called himself captain.

"Come." The captain swung on his officer. "What's happening?"

The first officer bowed. "We are under attack, Captain."

Rhys raised a single brow as he considered the man. "So I'd noticed. By whom?"

The youth mumbled a name. Just as Rhys had suspected, the Martian fleet had fallen to squabbling among themselves.

"Right!"

"We – " he cleared his throat – "the crew were wondering if you would return to the bridge, please."

And Rhys was moving before the young man had a chance to complete the request, brushing past him, shouting commands.

He clapped the young man on his back. "All right, mister! Let's see if we can break some heads."

Helmsman Delta of the *Revenant* had just taken over the command from his evening shift counterpart. He yawned and rubbed his eyes. It had been months since he'd worked aboard ship, and he had forgotten how fatiguing it was watching stationary stars. The tension of battle-ready status at all times was also taking its toll. He far preferred the nice, tidy war of the past, with battles that came at regularly scheduled intervals and periods of reprieve in between. This waiting for something to happen was ridiculous.

Delta glanced at the captain and then turned to stare at the endless vista of twinkling stars. And it seemed just for a second there that one of them stirred ever so slightly.

Delta hunched forward in his chair and squinted.

There it was again. Movement. He was sure of it.

The helmsman keyed in the scan sequence. The computer replied, printing out the make and model.

Peregrine-style craft, Martian manufacture, *circa* 2315. Unlike their Terran counterparts, the Martians preferred to name their craft after birds, especially birds of prey.

"Captain," he said, "enemy vessel at 4 o'clock."

A siren sounded. *Ar-ar-ar-ar-arg!* It rolled and resounded, on and on and on and on. And Blast was clawing her way from sleep as heavy and as dense as any black hole.

And on!

She batted at the place over to her right where her chrono alarm should be and hit a pan. It fell clattering to the floor.

"What the—" Ylon's voice sounded thick and heavy with sleep.

The light went on, and only then did she notice her cramped posture, curled up on the cold, hard floor. She opened her eyes to find herself nose to nose with a meat cleaver that was hanging on a rack next to her head.

Using a counter as her lever, she dragged herself on to her feet. She scratched her tummy, peering owlishly at Ylon on the far side of the kitchen.

The alarm klaxoned, jarring her senses and dulling her wits, so it took a moment before she recognized

Dirk, standing in the middle of the room, looking more than a bit silly with his mouth half ajar and a banana hanging out of it.

T he servo-mech had never been so happy – if such a term can be applied to a droid – at any time in its thirty-year history. The ship was busy and bustling with life. Robbie enjoyed all the activity, and it was called upon to serve here, there and everywhere.

Robbie felt needed.

And during those rare times when the lounge was unoccupied – late at night when all that could slept while others performed their duties – the robot could sit and contemplate the stars, undisturbed. Then Robbie would watch the dull ochre glow of the planet growing in the distance and match the stars against the maps of the constellations in AWS's memory banks, until passengers and crew would again descend during the designated daytime period, to dawdle and dither away the hours as they waited their arrival at Mars or recall to Earth.

All of this – the human crowd, the eternal stellar night – was still new to Robbie. The robot had yet to digest the concept of space or universe. So the servo-mech was only moderately startled when one of the stars began to move and grow, but then Robbie had also noticed that Mars likewise grew point-o-o-o-nine per cent each day. This star was expanding with alarming rapidity and seemed to create a ripple in space as it passed, leaving a tail of distortion in its wake.

It was, Robbie decided, a funny shape.

The robot's wonder deepened to disquiet as the alarms began to scream. It played with its auditory controls, modulating out the higher tones and then fiddled with its volume receptors until the noise became a muffled buzz.

The star changed in its configuration as it advanced and became clearer, and the tiny droid recognized it now as a vessel, like the one upon which they rode.

Just then the *Revenant* veered. The droid jounced sideways, and people came pouring into the hall.

Robbie gave a squawk of disappointment at their intrusion, for now the droid would have to quit the lounge and give up its fascinating examination of the sky.

It took a second before the alarm's meaning registered. The *Revenant* was under attack!

Blast had heard such klaxons, in battle and in drill, many times before in her life. At one time it would not have startled her. Then it had been as much a part of daily living as breathing or using the sanitary facilities.

A moment later, Blast reacted, and her heart sank. It was a sound she had hoped she would never hear again.

Blast and Ylon exchanged glances, and Blast knew Ylon felt the same way.

Meanwhile, Dirk bit and chewed. The end of the banana fell from his lips.

Splat!

The siren yammered on, and the absurdity of the situation hit her. There was a very real possibility that they could die, and there was Dirk caught with a banana in his mouth. Inexplicable merriment bubbled up in her and she started to giggle.

The ship tacked sharply. The clones, used to space travel, compensated. Dirk was thrown against the counter and began to choke, turning a lovely shade of purple. Ylon scrambled to Dirk's aid, twittering as he skirted the many barricades of kitchen counters, table tops, stoves and sleeping drones.

The youth spat and huddled, shoulders heaving, trying to catch his breath. The klaxon shut off. Ylon froze. Blast stared at the speaker.

Dirk straightened and tried to recover what he

could of his lost dignity by facing them head-on, feet wide, arms crossed.

"I'm not going back," he said, using his height to best advantage, staring down on them.

The incongruity of the youth's situation merged with the relief she felt that the alarm had proven false, and Blast's giggles erupted into guffaws. She doubled over with laughter.

"What's so funny?" Dirk demanded, wounded by their mirth.

"You are," said Ylon between gasps.

"It would be a pretty undignified way to die in battle," said Blast, "with a banana dangling out of your mouth."

"Battle?" Dirk's voice rose an octave and cracked. "Oh, was that what that ruckus was all about? I never paid much attention to the alarms."

The two gave up any attempt at self-control and howled.

"I don't see what's so funny!" He paused as his brain switched from one gear to another. "Wait a second, what battle? Why would there be a battle? We are not at war."

The two Lilliputian clones sobered, fast. Blast wiped tears from her eyes.

Ylon gazed at Dirk. "You are lucky. If that had been a real alarm, you wouldn't have to worry about being found in that unseemly position." He pointed at the half-chewed banana. "You would have been vaporized."

Blast shook her head in wonder. "I find it incredible to believe that the director of Deep Space HQ, the former Galactic War Headquarters, doesn't even know that Earth is at war with its colony, Mars. If you hadn't absconded from your post—"

"What? Earth is at war? I knew something was going on – things weren't happening according to plan – but I didn't realize ..." His voice dwindled and he examined his hands.

Dirk leaned against a counter. "I guess I have been a little out of touch lately."

"I'll say!" said Ylon.

"What I want to know is, what could have possibly possessed you to leave your post?" asked Blast.

Dirk shrugged.

"By the way," said Ylon, "where's—"

An awful racket drowned out the rest of his question. Blast jumped as a drone swung into action, lumbering straight for her. She belly-flopped, sliding under a table, just in time. It continued on towards Dirk. She spun on her belly and wondered if they had been found out.

Gwen loped down the circular shaft like an old hand. Now that she had been in residence for a while, she had decided that she liked this deep underbelly of the ship. She liked the solitude and being able to walk from one end of the vessel to another without being accosted by the other inhabitants, and she liked seeing how things worked.

Gwen resolved that wherever she might end up she was going to apply for an engineering apprenticeship. She wanted to be one of the ones crawling along the outside of a vessel, putting things together. She didn't want to be stuck behind a desk like her father was.

Wherever she might end up. Gwen grimaced at the thought, for she had heard the clangour of alarms and recognized them for what they were. She fully intended to find somebody, anybody, and ask what in heaven's name was going on.

Through her work with Ylon and Blast, Gwen knew enough about the proposed voyage to know that drills and alerts were not part of the schedule. Weapons had been provided for use at their final destination, so that they could hunt to supplement their food supplies or in the awful eventuality that they met up with hostiles upon their arrival.

The captains may have implemented drill in order to keep both equipment and crew in top form, in which case Gwen was going to be giving up her freedom for nothing, for she expected to be sent to the brig for her audacity.

But all the evidence – from the issuing of sidearms to the alarms – pointed to belligerents much closer to home. The sharp tack that had thrown her against the wall implied an evasive manoeuvre, such as might be encountered when dodging a shot. She rubbed her bruised elbow.

No, Gwen frowned. It was not a drill.

She slowed her pace. Nothing had gone according to the plan. They were days behind schedule – so many days, she had lost count. Gwen had hoped they'd be halfway to Alpha Centauri before she revealed her presence. They should have been by now.

Whatever had happened the Lilliputs were quite unprepared for it, caught on the hop, and that was not like them.

No, something awful was happening, and she had to find out what it was even if it meant spending the rest of the trip in confinement.

Where her voyage would end, she could only guess. Mars, most likely, with an eventual return to the orbital and her father's care until she reached legal age in a few months' time. Her scowl deepened. She would only try it again.

At least Gwen could comfort herself that, at the rate they were progressing, it would take a while before they achieved Martian orbit, giving her plenty of time to plead her case.

She rounded another bend, and a plaid-like network of light spilled across the shaft. She'd reached the grill to the kitchen.

Steeling herself, Gwen took a deep breath, wiped

the sweat from her hands and grasped the metal lattice. She thrust it into the room, heedless of the clatter. What did it matter if she was caught? She was giving herself up anyway.

The grill fell, hitting a kitchen droid. The drone shot forward.

"Nothing like entering with a bang," she muttered as she crouched down to crawl through the vent and found herself staring into the face of a clone.

"Blast!"

"Gwen!" Hands reached through and dragged her from the shaft.

The girl spun to regard Dirk. Her face fell.

Ylon moved between the two of them. "We have been looking for the two of you for a couple of weeks."

"What are you doing here?" Dirk said to Gwen.

"What are *you* doing here?" Her tone was accusatory.

Dirk blanched and studied his feet.

They all spoke at once. Behind them the droid rocked back and forth, performing some unknown function.

A whistle cut through the pandemonium. They turned to Blast. She reached over and switched off the drone.

"First things first. We'll find out who's been doing what to whom, and where," she glowered at the two of them, somehow managing to take in both of them with her glare despite the fact that they were located in different areas of the kitchens. "Later, after we find out what's going on elsewhere."

Her eyes locked on her partner. "Ylon, don't you think we should call in and find out what the alert was all about?"

"Yes," rasped Gwen, "I was coming to find out about that."

Ylon cut her off with a slicing motion across his throat. He murmured something in his comm-unit, hesitating as he listened. A few minutes later, he signed off, his expression pensive. The other three converged upon him.

"Yes?" Blast said.

"A Martian ship approached."

Blast waited for Ylon to proceed. Dirk frowned while Gwen merely looked bewildered.

"Although it was carrying the Earth flag, or a version of it hastily painted over the Mars logo, the vessel was definitely of Martian make and design. And armed for battle."

Blast nodded. One of the many more adventurous types that had found their homes on Mars were pirates. They thrived there, where they could not have flourished anywhere else on the more civilized trade routes. So all Martian freighters, cargo carriers and traders were equipped with weaponry, weaponry illegal on most vessels of that type. Blast wouldn't be at all surprised if some of them had cloaking devices.

The news explained the alarm, but it did not explain its cancellation.

"Yes?" Dirk goaded.

"It's our escort."

"A Martian escort?"

"Military escort", Ylon paused as he assimilated the information, "from Earth."

"Earth? In a Martian vessel?" said Blast.

"Wait a second," Gwen interrupted. "What is all this about Mars? What's wrong with them sending an escort to their new Lilliputian settlers?"

"Mars and Earth are at war," Dirk informed her.

And Gwen's legs gave out from under her.

He caught her and lifted her up to a counter. She blushed, eyes averted, and grinned sheepishly at the two clones. "I haven't eaten since yesterday. I guess I'm a little hungry."

"Ah, yes, well, we're having something of our own little food crisis here," explained Blast.

"We've noticed," said Dirk, and he shuffled nervously away from Gwen. "Say, what happened there? You were supposed to go straight to—"

Ylon finished his statement for him. "You mean, leap into the arms of the enemy?"

"Ah, yes, well, I guess it makes sense that you delayed; but why are Mars and Earth at war?"

"Because of us, or the land granted to our people," said Blast. She explained hastily.

"We'd rather hoped that they'd have everything

ironed out by now." Blast sighed. "I suppose we'll have to fight eventually."

"Not if I have anything to say about it," mumbled Dirk.

"I don't suppose you'll have much to say about anything." Blast looked at Dirk out of the corner of her eye. "You're not supposed to be on the *Revenant*. Remember? You may be head of DSHQ on Earth, but here you're just a runaway, and we have no idea what the captains will decide to do with you."

"Put us in the brig," suggested Gwen.

Blast studied the girl's face. "Not very likely. I mean, it isn't as if you can run away from here." Her arm swept expansively, taking in the entire ship. "Where can you go?"

"Back to where they came from," snapped Ylon. "Which reminds me, where *did* you come from?"

The two stared into opposite corners of the room, stubbornly silent.

Blast ogled the pair. "You don't mean to tell me that neither of you knew about the other?"

"What about Robbie?" said Ylon.

For the first time, Dirk met Ylon's gaze. "Robbie?"

"He's missing too."

Dirk's head wagged from side to side, arms out, palms up, to indicate they were empty. "He's not with me. I haven't seen him."

"He's obviously followed you. Robbie's not creative enough to come up with this idea on his own. We can only hope that now that you're captured, he'll turn up. The more important question is: what are we two going to do with you?" Ylon said.

"Feed them, first," said Blast.

"What about the rations?"

"What do you expect the kids to do? Starve for the duration of the trip? Besides we didn't eat dinner last night; we came straight here from shift. They can have our rations."

"I brought supplies," Dirk said defensively.

Ylon winked at Blast as she hustled about the kitchen, putting her plan into action. "See, I told you he'd plan ahead."

"Did I argue?" She roused a droid from its silicon slumber and ordered breakfast. She rounded up four others and instructed them to line up in a row before the counter.

"Voilà!" she said. "Table and chairs."

The drone brought over a steaming tray.

"Eggs," announced Blast.

Dirk groaned. He had plenty of the dried variety in his stores. If these things had ever seen the inside of a chicken, he'd eat his hat. He snorted. Come to think of it, his hat would probably taste better.

Gwen piped up. "So, what are you going to do with us?"

"We've been debating that for quite some time", said Ylon, "without really coming to a conclusion. When we first heard about you, Dirk," he stabbed his fork at the youth, "we both resolved to send you home. You don't seem to understand that you would not just be leaving home and family behind, but your entire species. There would be no one of your own kind with whom you could form a relationship."

"That's a specist statement to make," grumbled Dirk.

"But true," Blast said gently. "If you were to remain with us, you could never", her eyes flicked to Gwen, "for example, marry or have a family of your own."

Blast took a mouthful of eggs, chewed thoughtfully, swallowed and continued. "Then we learned about you, Gwen, and we thought you two had made your decision together. Matters of legalities aside, suddenly the issue wasn't nearly so cut and dried as it first appeared."

Her eyes found Ylon's. "And with Martian war, it's getting murkier even still. I think that the captains are too busy to deal with you right now, and we've been ordered by Earth to maintain radio silence."

Ylon scoffed. "As if it wasn't standard operating procedure."

"Yes, well, I wish they hadn't been quite so rigid about their orders," added Blast. "It would have been nice to know about our escort. Stupid idiots should have warned us a ship was coming. They could have got us all killed."

"The Martians' ship radio was out."

"Oh." Blast mouthed the word. "That explains our escort not advising us of their approach, but what about Earth? The only calls we have received are about you, from Council Members Alexander and Moor. Using security override, of course."

Dirk winced.

"My father?" queried Gwen.

"That was Council Member Moor," Ylon said. "Your father, ah, doesn't have the authority to break the communication ban."

She swallowed hard and studied the eggs on her plate.

"That still doesn't tell us what we should do with you," commented Ylon. "I agree with Blast. I think Cyte, Zygote and Zed have enough on their hands. That gives you something of a reprieve, I guess. I for one am tired and would like to get some sleep before the beginning of our shift, and I think you two have a lot to think about."

"The problem remains," said Blast, "where to put them. We can't hide you in our quarters. We're sleeping in shifts and only have access to our rooms eight hours out of every twenty-four."

"Of that eight hours," Ylon checked his chronometer, "we have only a few left."

"We could return to our digs," Dirk hinted helpfully.

"And disappear in the bowels of the ship where we can't find you? No, sir," said Ylon.

"Don't you trust us enough to tell us where you've been?" Blast addressed her question to Gwen.

"Yes."

Dirk shouted and threw up his hands as Gwen fished a compu-cube from her pocket.

"Computer, map," commanded Gwen. The line drawings of the ship appeared with the route high-lighted and the position of her hide-out pinpointed.

Ylon was amazed. "You mean there's that much wasted space on this ship? We could have used it as a room."

"It's occupied," asserted Gwen.

"Oh, right."

They swung to Dirk. He set his chin and crossed his arms.

"Do you trust us any less than Gwen?" Blast reproved.

He softened and explained to them how to get to his den.

"In the maintenance corridors?" Ylon stroked his moustache. "You took a risk."

"Not really. Only droids go down there."

"Well, I'm glad we didn't keep up the search. It would have taken ages for us to find you."

"Now, if we can only solve the mystery of Rob-bie," said Blast.

"Robbie?" said Dirk. "He's not here. Robbie would only come if he were following me, and don't you think I'd know it!" His face darkened as he recalled the moved boxes and the tidied books. His mouth dropped open in dawning realization.

Blast noted his expression and remarked, "Just as I thought. He's around, all right. You just haven't seen him."

Rhys did two things as he swung into the captain's seat. He demanded a channel open on a broad band to all ships and ordered blanket fire – fore, aft, starboard and port. Any vessel within range, combatant or non-combatant, would be grazed.

That would grab their attention.

"Now hear this! This is your duly elected leader, Rhys Gordon, ordering an immediate ceasefire."

The silence by which the fleet responded was profound. Rhys relaxed in his chair when he saw that no more shots had been fired for a full five minutes. They hadn't called his bluff.

"Now there's this little matter about my alleged treason." One small quadrant of the comm-screen brightened and a dusty-faced captain peered at Rhys. Before the other man could speak, Rhys continued: "Did I not say that we must consolidate our efforts or we would accomplish nothing?"

Another face appeared to stare at him, tight-lipped. Behind the captain, fire flickered and cabin crew fought the flames.

"And what is happening now?" he roared.

More ship captains opened a return line and more faces appeared on his screen.

"Is this how you consolidate your efforts? Is this how you plan to defeat planet Earth, by killing yourselves off one by one? An novel approach, of which I'm sure your opponents will approve."

The screen was completely filled and the over-loaded comm-line circuit hissed and squawked.

"Or", he finished reasonably, "do we get together and draw up a plan of action? Gentlemen, which do you prefer? I await your decision, over and out."

He pointed at the communications officer, and the screen blanked out just before the babble reached pandemonium proportions.

17/9/2334

O-nine-hundred Hours

A red-eyed pair had checked in for the beginning of the shift. Blast grimaced an apology to their commander and looked away, afraid that the news of last night's discovery might be reflected in her eyes.

A sympathetic Ylon inclined his head towards her. Neither felt completely comfortable keeping secrets from their commanding officer. The captain returned his attention to his nightshift counterpart Cyte, who was completing his narrative of last night's events.

Ylon sat behind the communications system control panel and logged in the date and the shift. He began standard equipment checks and leafed through the log, empty of all save one entry. With the escort ship's radio out, it had been a telegraphed message, with the text tapped out, using the not-quite-lost art of Morse code.

Without the stimulation provided by continual contact with the outside world, their work-shift was boring indeed. Ylon's eyes devoured the communique – the first in many days – as the former shift officer recited it verbatim.

"Someone was sent over to their escort craft to repair their communications console."

"Lucky bloke!" muttered Ylon.

"It is fixed, and they are maintaining radio-silence."

"Figures," said Blast.

If it hadn't been for the excitement of finding Dirk and Gwen, Ylon would've died of terminal tedium.

And the so-called war. Which wasn't a war, not really. No battles had been fought. So far as Ylon knew, the opposing forces had never met. "Is there no other news of Earth?" he asked.

"No," said the Upsilon male.

Ylon grimaced. What had begun as a communications blackout had effectively become a news blackout.

Blast huffed and hunkered down in her chair. "Earth could have been destroyed and Mars emerged victorious, and no one aboard ship would know about it."

"Read the ship's logs if you want the latest," said the nightshift man.

Blast keyed in the report. The nightshift man patted the back of her chair. "I'm off to get some kip."

"Sounds good." Ylon yawned, performing the early morning checks perfunctorily. He slumped in his chair and stared blankly at the wall of screens. Beside him, Blast took over the systems' checks without missing a beat.

The bridge layout for the Manta was identical to that of the Orca-style cruiser, except for its size. The forward section of the circular bridge was dominated by a series of smaller screens which, used singly, could provide a full three-hundred-and-sixty-degree view around the ship or, used as one unit, could provide a magnificent panoramic vista.

It was the latter image that was projected now. It would have been a spectacular scene if he hadn't been looking at it for the last four days. The only changes were a slight enlargement of Mars and the occasional flickering of the escort on to their viewscreens.

Helmsman Kappa emitted something like a squeak.

Captain Zed glanced up, annoyed, from his conversation with Cyte.

"We have company, Captain," Kappa said. "One up close and a large battalion farther away."

Captain Zed stepped down from his chair and walked closer to the screen.

"Position of the squadron?"

"Northwest quadrant, sector fourteen."

"Can we get a visual?" asked Zed.

"Not of the fleet, but I can show you the approaching ship."

Meanwhile Captain Cyte was fiddling with the arm controls, switching from screen to screen to screen. Cold, brittle stars winked blandly back at them, secure in their fixed positions in the heavens. The view froze, and Ylon craned his neck to stare at the tiny sparkle of light that flitted in defiance of the stellar map.

The captain called for a scan of the vessel.

"I'm already on that," said Kappa. "It appears to be of Lunar make, but there's something odd about the configuration. I can't put my finger on it."

"Xi," Zed bellowed at the Chief Technical Officer, "check the system. See if anything is wrong with it."

Zed questioned the helmsman. "Could it be armed?"

Captain Zed returned to stand next to his twin, Cyte. "By the sun, moon and stars, if they've sent another escort without notifying us..."

Cyte sniffed in disdainful accord. "I don't think they know how to run a war without us."

Xi spoke. "I'm sorry, I can't tell much. The scanning equipment's not that sensitive. It was never designed for internal scans."

All eyes turned to the screen. Oh, for the good old days when battles were predicted and predictable!

When all equipment fell into certain categories with armaments regulated by law, restricted to certain models and makes. There was no need for sophisticated scans of equipment.

Since the deregulation following the peace, owners and captains made modifications when and where they could. As always, government regulations had yet to reflect the change in man's circumstances. Improvements and upgrades were often cobbled together, piecemeal. This had resulted in a change of the modern spelling from piecemeal to peace-meal. A word that carried within its context the connotation of not only shoddy workmanship, but also of the privation and want that had accompanied the peace.

"I think, though," said Xi, "I could modify it . . . if I recalibrate the—"

"Very good, Xi. Do what is necessary, but see if you can give me a more accurate picture of the other ship's capabilities."

Part of the screen dissolved – or the stars upon it did – and a line drawing appeared, with model specifications and requirements printed on the left.

"That's the normal design. This", he keyed something and a hazy grey outline materialized to the right, "is the vessel. Note the hump."

Cyte snapped his fingers. "A gun turret."

"I don't know that yet. However, if I can increase the rate of ion bombardment we should get better penetration into the hull and we may be able to get an inside view of the ship. Superficially, that is. Since that is a superficial feature, something that has been riveted on to the exterior, it should suffice."

"You don't need to scan." Cyte hurrumphed. "It's a gun turret if I've ever seen one."

"There, we've got it!" Xi shouted. "A gun, definitely, but they're still too far away for us to distinguish what kind."

"Open a hailing frequency."

Blast, a little bit quicker than Ylon, responded.

Zed paced in front of the screen. He opened his mouth to speak.

Another screen opened, borrowing a little from the view of space and the ship's specification. An angry human face glowered down at Zed.

"Must I remind you there is a radio blackout?"

"Forget the blackout. We need to know if that is friend or foe." Zed jabbed a finger at the ship.

"We are in a state of war. We must assume it is an enemy vessel."

"The craft is Lunar; it could be another escort."

The man drawled. "We have not been informed of another escort."

"Must I remind you there is a communications blackout?" Zed quipped, modulating the deeper human tones note for note. "Might I also remind you that if we had taken that attitude with your arrival, we would probably not be having this conversation right now, because we would have blasted you to smithereens and asked questions later."

The man's expression tightened. "We are your escort. It is our responsibility to defend you against all eventualities."

"Even amicable advances."

"Signing off." The face vanished.

"What do you want me to do, Captain?" Blast said.

Xi continued to mutter and splutter in the background. "Tweak a little power here ..."

"I suppose we should wait until the vessel comes closer. Perhaps it will identify itself and give our escort a chance to get lost among the stars." Zed climbed back on his seat.

"I don't think they will be so obliging," Cyte said. The first officer relinquished his chair to the nightshift captain. "Good lad. He knows I'm not likely to go anywhere just when things are starting to happen."

Zed spoke to the first officer, and to Cyte. "I think we should be prepared for anything. I don't trust our escort here not to attack a friendly vessel, blowing up themselves, and us too, in the process."

Cyte looked pensive. "They could surprise us, though, and be right. That may be an enemy vessel."

"Helmsman," ordered Zed, "battle-ready status. Shields up. Arm the ship, and be ready to take evasive action."

A yellow light began flashing.

"Xi, you'll have to forget about the equipment

now. I need you to calculate a defensive leap." Zed caught Cyte's eye. "But recalibrate to include the weight and volume displacement of the escort vessel. We're going to catch her in our tractor beam and drag her out of harm's way." Zed sighed. "They are our allies, after all."

The tanker trundled on, unaware of the furore it was causing. It filled their screen, leaving no doubt about its make and model, or alleged affiliation, and still no word.

"Unless the crew are under specific orders of silence, they should have contacted us by now. Open a hailing frequency, but close down all other channels beyond the band extended to the Lunar ship. I don't want to be interrupted this time."

Ylon completed the first part of the command, as Blast flicked a series of switches to the off position, effectively cutting off all frequencies.

"This is *HMS Revenant* en route to Mars. Please identify yourself, Lunar vessel."

The escort tried to break through. The screen became scrambled, and the Lunar vessel's approach was obscured.

Ylon attacked the switches.

"... leave ... *crackle* ... off ... back off ... *sizzle* ... we shall attack!"

The Lunar vessel must have been monitoring all the frequencies, for it swerved from the sedate parallel course it had been following to its port side, as a shot from the newly rechristened *Alliance I* went wide.

"Sound alert."

The klaxon whooped in the background.

Ignoring the motley escort, the Lunar ship spun and headed straight for *Revenant*. Clearly, the other vessel wasn't interested in their escort.

"Are you ready, Xi?"

"Aye, sir!"

"Grab the *Alliance*."

A cone of blue white light pierced the night, reaching toward the Martian-cum-Terran cargo carrier.

The alarm shrieked with an increased urgency. The enemy ship had armed itself.

A milk-white blast issued from the enemy ship.

Ylon inhaled. To the observer, space battle had a beauty, with its flashes of bright light that spanned the heavens. Each shot used all colours of the spectrum, from white close to its base and descending through the rainbow from yellow to violet the further vapour fire got from its point of origin.

Dusky purple light by-passed their ship.

Gone were the bullets, blood and gore of yesteryear. There were no faces, no names. One could almost forget about death. Almost, thought Ylon, and he began to sweat when, a minute later, a second blast followed the first.

Captains Zed and Cyte strained forward in their

seats, urging the beam to its mark. The *Revenant* would not have time to see if their tractor had found its target.

"Helmsman, leap!" bawled Zed. "Now!"

The flat black darkness of ultra-space surrounded them. They were intact and whole. The escort was nowhere in sight.

Zed exhaled softly, relaxed, and surveyed his crew with pride. They remained in the rigid postures of attention.

The ship's computer counted out loud.

"One. Two. Three."

The stars reformed, wriggling into place with a motion that caused one's stomach to churn. But worse than that was the sight of twisted wreckage that floated where the Martian ship used to be.

Everyone sat in stunned silence and stared.

The flotsam glowed with the heat of its ignition, the flames extinguished by the vacuum of space.

Ylon's head snapped on his neck and he spun to the viewscreens, searching for either their enemy or their escort.

A mewled choking noise came from Blast's throat. She pointed shakily to a portion of mangled hull that bore Earth's flag, painted over the Martian logo.

"The detritus appears to be the remains of a ship of Martian design," Xi announced impartially.

Zed leapt to his feet, shouting, "The enemy?

Where's the enemy ship? Give me a full-three-hun-dred-and-sixty-degree view."

The Lunar vessel wallowed in space, listing to one side. It drifted dark and lifeless, apparently disabled.

"Report on the status of enemy ship," barked Zed.

"Engines are not only down, they're off. We don't get any readings from the craft at all. They're dead in the water, sir."

The image on the screen changed, as if somewhere within the vessel they sensed the scans were through, for light blazed across its bow as the ship sprung to life. There was a faint twinkle, or spark, as another shot was fired.

"Get us out of here!" Zed and Cyte roared in unison. "Leap! Take us back into ultra-space. Fast."

The shimmering detritus dissolved, as did the shot that had engulfed them, and velvety darkness replaced light.

"Captain? The tractor beam is still on."

Zed concentrated on the screen. "Well, like the first time, it didn't capture anybody. Did it?"

"Unless it slammed the ship against the wall of . . ." he floundered at a loss for words, "reality or time." Xi gave up helpless. "Whatever it is."

"You mean we could be the cause of all that destruction to the *Alliance*?"

The CTO's jaw tightened, a muscle jumped in his neck. "Should I take us back?"

Zed cocked his head and conferred with Cyte for a moment.

"No, I don't think so. If we were, in fact, the cause of all that," he gestured at the empty screen, "then the other ship is likewise destroyed. If not, we can be pretty sure that the Lunar vessel will be waiting for us."

The helmsman kept his finger poised over the keyboard. "Destination?"

"Calculate the jump to Mars."

"Captain?"

"Not Mars itself, the opposite side of the planet approximately parallel to our position now. HQ wants us to go slow. Fine. We'll go slow, but nobody said from which direction we might approach."

Zed jabbed his finger at a place on the stellar map. "Take us here, as far from Mars as we are now, but on the antipodal side. Let's see if we can give them a little surprise."

"Lieutenant Ylon, as soon as we have returned to normal space, I think it's about time we broke radio silence. We must inform DSHQ what has happened here today. It would appear that the Moon has finally taken sides in this conflict."

Blast keyed in the message while Ylon typed in the enemy vessel's alpha-numeric designation and double-checked them.

"Wait to send until we have reached normal

space, and bounce it off everything you can find. I don't want anyone to know where we are.

"Come on, helmsman, let's move. I don't want to find out that another one of the Lunar modifications includes star drive."

There was a sensation, similar to a lurch but without physical movement, as if the bottom had dropped out from under them, that signalled the *Revenant* had achieved forward motion in the void of ultra-space.

Excitement past, the lounge emptied at the change of shifts. It was still empty as people ate and bathed and wound their way to their respective assignments. Robbie returned, but the servo-mech knew it was safe for a little while only. After breakfast, those without assigned duties or quarters would start to filter into the chamber once more.

Still fascinated, the servo-mech could not tear itself away from the glass as it learned more about each individual star. Already Robbie had worked his way through the visible quadrant and identified the major constellations and the planetary bodies. Now it was eager for a different perspective of the universe.

In anticipation of the first of the morning arrivals, the machine compacted itself, withdrawing its tentacle arms behind the skirt of the apron and lowering itself on its air-cushioned shock absorbers so its wheels were barely visible.

Clack. Splat. Burp. Wheeze. Ahhhhh.

Robbie was doing a passing fair imitation of a table. The servo-mech had just opened the file on Mars itself and had found a surfeit of information. Beyond the standard data of "dimensions, density, mass, rotation, and velocity", it had a government, a history, and whole plethora of legal documentation, land grants, and alliance treaties.

Robbie was delighted. The servo-mech was not even mildly curious when the other ship appeared on the scene. This was the second craft in a relatively short period. Obviously, they were not alone in this universe.

With its newly expanded perspective of the galaxy and its structure, Robbie noted the logo and saw that it was that of the Moon.

The droid was continuing to peruse the material on Mars when the sky outside it exploded into shards of colour and light. The photoreceptor cells pivoted. Robbie tooted.

The next thing the robot knew the starscape had vanished as if somebody had snuffed it out or covered it behind a thick black curtain. Before this event had been fully grasped and assimilated by the hapless droid, the stars reappeared, starting as oscillating dots that solidified into the more familiar map. The little robot swayed dizzily.

Then it took in the melting pieces of metal, the charred chunks of nose cone and strut, the fragments of hull. Robbie watched as the other ship powered up and came swooping down upon the *Revenant*.

Rising slightly, Robbie bleated a warning to anyone who would listen. Light leached the stars from the heavens and was swiftly replaced by soothing blackness.

Robbie settled with a relieved whoosh and waited for the sky to return, preferably a clean and pristine sky without debris or offending ship.

And Robbie waited.

And waited.

And waited.

Someone had stolen the sky away.

The first of the morning's passengers entered the lounge. The servo-mech did not budge. Having just discovered the heavens, Robbie wanted to see it again. Make sure it was real. Make sure it existed. Make sure that it was there.

Had the servo-mech missed a vital entry? That this was just fiction, like the holo-casts that appeared in the living room?

Could anything as vast as a universe just vanish?

More passengers filtered into the chamber.

Robbie shivered.

The room had become quite crowded when the sky again melted into focus, and Robbie was delighted. The servo-mech trilled. The retractor arms emerged from behind the apron and clapped at the rediscovered universe.

Then Robbie noticed that Mars had moved from one side of the stellar map to the other and many of the constellations were new.

Robbie squawked, overjoyed that its wish had been granted, when a hand tapped the robot on a metal shoulder.

"Hey, you! I've been looking for you."

Technician Psi stalked irritably through the lounge. She had nowhere to go. Her shift had just ended, and it was still not her assigned sleep period, so her living quarters were off limits.

But she could not have slept if she wanted to. She was still wired, and after this morning's events, Psi doubted she'd be able to sleep even when her time came.

She moved up to the window and stood, gazing out at the nothingness. This ship, she assured herself, could beat anything currently in the skies.

However, Psi thought as Mars reformed in a different quadrant, the captain had the right idea. Make 'em work for the battle they so desired.

"Good," she muttered. "Let them try and find us now."

"Clatter! Warble!"

The technician spun, spied the floral drape on the box and darted between passengers and crew to bang on the metal back.

"Hey, you! I've been looking for you."

A whistle of enquiry.

"And now I've found you," she said triumphantly as she clasped an arm, "and I'm going to take you to repair where you belong."

"Captain?"

Rhys looked up from the battle plan.

"The scout vessel has disappeared from our radar, and so has the *Revenant*. There's debris which, together with the bursts, seems to indicate a battle has taken place."

"And the *Revenant* destroyed?"

"I don't think so, sir. There's not enough rubble to account for the loss of both ships."

"Good. Scan the heavens. Get all orbitals, settlements and mining operations, and domestic fleet involved in the operation. She's out there somewhere, and we must try and find her."

17/9/2334

O-ten-thirty

FROM: NEWSNET INTERNATIONAL
DISTRIBUTION: UNIVERSAL
DATELINE: MARTIAN SPACE; 17/9/2334
SUBJECT: WAR HEATS UP

THE FIRST OFFICIAL ENGAGEMENT OF THE WAR RESULTED IN A DRAW. THE INCIDENT OCCURRED AT 08:00 THIS MORNING, WHEN THE ALLIANCE - RECENTLY CONFISCATED FROM A MARTIAN TRADER - MET AN OPPOSING VESSEL OF UNKNOWN MAKE. BOTH SHIPS WERE DESTROYED. UNCONFIRMED REPORTS CLAIM THAT THE ATTACKING VESSEL WAS LUNAR, GIVING RISE TO SERIOUS QUESTIONS ABOUT THE MOON'S ALLEGIANCES, PARTICULARLY AFTER THE TRADE DISPUTE EARLIER THIS YEAR THAT RESULTED IN THE PLANETARY FOOD CRISIS . . .

DURING AN EMERGENCY SESSION, CENTRAL COMMAND

The *Revenant* had glided into a slow orbit – if one could call moving in a wide loop outside Mars's territorial air space and that of its moons, an orbit – but the captains had no desire to give the Martians a reason to fight. From here, they could jump with ease to Mars and back, or maintain a discreet distance, as needed.

After their course was established, Cyte and Zed retreated to the captains' ready-room. They sat at the table and stared gloomily in front of them.

"I'm getting really tired of this," said Cyte. "Tired of waiting for battle."

Zed snorted. "We don't appear to have to wait for long, do we? We should be used to it."

"This is different," said Cyte. "Before we were prepared. We relied on ourselves and our equipment." He wrinkled his nose in disgust. "Now we are dependent upon rather faulty human logic, rather than the computer. As a result, we're sitting ducks while Earth decides what it's going to do."

"Well, do you have any strategies?" said Zed.

"It would be nice if the time and location of the next engagement were ours to choose."

"But how do we select a target? Do you suggest we hit civilians?"

178

"I'm beginning to wonder if there are any civilians in this conflict," said Zed.

"Humph. You've got a point there."

Zed grinned.

"What are you smiling about?" Cyte groused.

"Why don't we get Xi and the technicians working on embellishments to the scanning systems? Maybe then we can predict who is a friend and who is not."

"It would be helpful, but for now, I think it's a safe assumption that everybody who approaches is an enemy until proven otherwise."

Collared! Apprehended, captured, snatched, seized. A list of words new to the recently voder-enhanced robot flitted through the silicon circuits of the servo-mech's brain, and the gears whirled as Robbie searched around him for a means of escape. But the technician kept a hand firmly clamped on a metal retractor arm, towing Robbie along behind her, as she grumbled about stroppy robots and inconsiderate humans who didn't seem to know how to plan a simple relocation much less an interplanetary conquest.

Robbie noted that the woman's uniform was casually unbuttoned at the neck. From its experiences with Ylon and Blast, the servo-mech knew the Lilliputians well enough to realize that the tech was probably off-duty. No clone would be so informal on the job.

So the robot dropped computer-wipe from its list of immediate concerns and reconciled itself to its fate. It would follow the technician and flee later after the human left for its living quarters, shut down, or whatever humans did when they weren't working. For the servo-mech did not distinguish between the clones and their full-sized parents. One bi-pedal species was pretty much like another.

"Someone's oiled you!" The technician's tone was loud, denouncing the action as if it was treason.

The robot tooted in the affirmative and matched itself to the technician's gait.

Corpman Psi glowered at it. "Good. I won't have time for you till tomorrow."

They had traversed more than half the ship before Technician Psi released Robbie's arm to palm the ident pad that would let them into Engineering. The door slid noiselessly into the wall, to reveal another long hall punctuated by a series of glassed-in rooms. In each were tools and electrical equipment, oscilloscopes, and computers, some dismantled and some intact.

Robbie rolled past a room where a standard housekeeping droid – the upright variety – had been cleaved in two. Its wiring and circuitry were exposed, spilling in a tangle like viscera from its torso, as if the droid had been disembowelled.

The robot began to tremble. They reached one of

the maintenance cupboards. Psi pressed her hand to the plate. Robbie noticed a name written on the door.

She pulled a numbered tag from the peg on the wall and placed it on Robbie's back. Then Psi straightened and gazed at the many repair jobs strewn about the room. "I maybe not be able to get to you tomorrow either."

The quivering stopped.

The corpman studied Robbie. "Can I trust you to stay?"

This time there was no answering sound, neither beep, nor squawk, nor bleat.

She must've been losing her mind if she had attributed intelligence to this device. It had the wit neither to flee nor to reply. It was just a drone, after all, and Psi was exhausted. She'd report the droid's reappearance to her supervisor, then she'd go and get something to eat.

The woman rattled around in the closet for a few minutes, tidying and muttering under her breath. Then, with a gentle rap on Robbie's metal head, she departed.

The robot sat patiently, perusing those files that contained the history of Mars. Robbie had got as far as the original land grants and settlement charter, when the servo-mech decided it had waited long enough.

If the human was going to return for something it forgot, then it would have done so by now.

Robbie scooted forward cautiously, exchanged the standard three-pincer claw on its arm for a serial port, and plugged into the *Revenant*'s computers, searching for the code to release the locking mechanism. As the robot skimmed through the system, Robbie stumbled upon a file marked Mars and dumped it in a pilfered portion of AWS's memory for later scrutiny.

Once the servo-mech had located the code for the cubicle and outer doors, it completed a final scan of the environs with its heat-sensitive sensors before releasing the lock.

Robbie set the computer on timed-close and exited, careering up the hall. It barely paused to input the ident and was still tearing along as the doors retracted, and the servo-mech nearly bowled over a supply sergeant.

"Good!" he said as he stepped in front of the robot. "Helping hands. Just what the doctor ordered. Come with me, – I need you in cargo bay VI."

Morula's ship, the *Covenant*, hurtled through space. They were making good time. She glanced at the chronometer. Twenty-four hours into the voyage and already a third of the seventy million kilometres to Mars had been covered. But then Captain Morula had been ruthless, using everything, including jetsam, as an anchor to catapult her vessel through space, until her first officer had protested the ship couldn't stand the strain.

Still she squeezed every ounce of power from the engines, taking them to the limit, and then demanded more. For Morula was raring to go. She was sick of cruising hour upon hour through space, waiting for someone to misbehave. She was a warrior. She was made for action. She was ready for battle.

If she could just find it. The thwarted captain glared at the enlarged sector of the starscape where the *Revenant* had last been seen. Nothing except a large amount of free-floating matter consistent with the pattern found after the destruction of a vessel.

And in an adjacent sector, a fleet, heading away from the scene.

Morula could only hope that the junk didn't represent the *Revenant*, but the previous shift had witnessed what had appeared, from the flight patterns, to be a brief and abortive battle. And no ship remained from the encounter.

Morula wouldn't believe it, couldn't believe it. There wasn't enough debris for that large a ship. Still, her heart clenched tight when she thought of the people aboard, many of whom had been her former shipmates.

When she protested, her nightshift counterpart stated, "A vessel doesn't just disappear."

Morula squinted at the screen. "Really? Our ships can, if we jump into ultra-space."

"Only for a short period of time, as you well know," he advised.

"Ah, but we're talking about the *Revenant*. She was designed to do precisely that – leap for long periods. The only craft in the entire fleet that has that capability. For all we know they could have decided to steer clear of the conflict and jump straight to Alpha Centauri, taking passengers and crew with them."

The nightshift captain grunted. He'd given his report; if the dayshift commander chose to cherish a false hope about her mates, who was he to stop her? He left the bridge.

"OK, crew," she said, "let's get this bucket of bolts to Mars. I want to investigate the scene of battle before the larger chunks of rubble get caught by the gravitational pull and orbit to the antipodal side of the planet."

The helmsman peered down at her impassively. "I've got us going at top speed, Captain."

She fumed. The problem was that they'd left the civilized sector of space behind and now cruised beyond the Lunar belt where the numbers of auto-mated tankers, freighters and satellite relays that could be utilized as a catapult dwindled. The war followed by the edict against interplanetary travel ensured that even the most greedy merchant stayed at home, tucked snugly in his bed. Thus, the typical passenger flights were cancelled.

"Captain!"

She spun in her seat to face the CTO.

"We're picking up a ship on the opposite side of the planet. Do you think it might be the *Revenant*?"

Footsteps, a grumbling voice and the slight rumble of wheels alerted Gwen to yet another incursion into the cargo bays. She must've been crazy to think that the hold would be unpopulated.

She swore. She couldn't have picked a busier locale if she'd set up camp in the middle of the staff lounge.

Gwen held her breath and listened. Then she leaned back and exhaled with a sigh of relief.

At least this time it was a lone male and a not-particularly-well-functioning droid, judging by the number of expletives that were flying about.

They proceeded into the next cargo bay.

Great! A meeting had been scheduled with Ylon, Blast and Dirk here at the end of the shift. Gwen would have to leave and warn the Lilliputs.

Although she had several hours yet, there was no time like the present. She didn't want to get caught as she had in the past, and who knows if others might arrive? Gwen tried to remember what was stored in that particular bay. Was she facing another major disruption like before?

Gwen slipped the panel from its position in the wall and crept through. She hesitated long enough to orient her position from that of the clones.

"Look, you go over there and do a tally."

Silence.

"No, don't dust it. Just count. You can count, can't you?

"What are you wearing that apron for? You look ridiculous. Trust me to pick a droid with a cleanliness fetish!" The crewman kept up a continuous diatribe of complaints and invectives.

"Don't rearrange the boxes. They look just fine."

Gwen chuckled, gliding from shadow to shadow until she'd reached the ventilation shaft. She didn't know who she felt sorrier for – the man or the drone.

Now what? she thought. She couldn't just hang about for hours.

And Gwen knew where she could find refuge if she sought it. She froze. What would she say to Dirk? How could she explain her behaviour? She hadn't meant to hurt him, and now it would appear that she had.

Clang!

"You stupid droid! I said inventory, not tidy up! Get back here!"

Footsteps pounded down the hall and stopped just outside the hatch.

"I should've guessed you were in for repairs. I'm gonna make sure you have your memory wiped."

There was a suspiciously familiar squeak. Her ears pricked. The footsteps retreated, and the decision was made. She crab-walked to the place where she could stand erect and then slunk off into the darkness, heading for the complex of maintenance tunnels in the occupied portion of the ship.

Dirk prowled through his den like a caged animal. Never before had it seemed so much like a cell. He could neither rest nor sleep.

Because *she* was here. Just on the other side of the ship. All he had to do was walk out that door and. . .

He counted the steps. "One, two, three." He pivoted.

. . . talk to her, see her. . .

The youth retraced his steps to the far wall and back again.

. . . find out what was wrong. . .

He stopped, ran his index finger over the top of a box, rubbed it against his thumb and grimaced.

And Robbie was here too. Or so it seemed.

One, two, three. Turn. One, two, three, four. Out the door and turn. . .

"Oh!" Gwen huddled just outside his door, clearly as startled to see him as he had been to find her.

She shot him a sheepish grin.

He collapsed against the wall. "You frightened me. I was just coming –" and Dirk brightened –" to see you."

"You don't mind if I visit you, do you?"

"Of course not." He stepped back into his lair, letting her pass.

Gwen glanced around, lips pursed, and she nodded sharply. "You did come prepared, didn't you?"

He shrugged.

"I didn't. I should have. I think stowing away was in the back of my mind all along." Gwen peeked at him out of the corner of her eye. "You were planning to go along too, and not tell me." It was a statement, not a question.

He looked hurt. "No, of course not." Dirk stuffed his hands in his pockets. "Well, maybe at first. You were so upset at what your father had done, the blemish to the family honour. You could tell you came from a solid military background. I thought if I told you I was going to throw all responsibilities, protocol and family honour aside and jump ship – well, I didn't know how you'd react."

"Me neither."

"And just when I was sure of you, you started giving me the cold shoulder."

Gwen let loose with a short, sharp bark of laughter.

He lifted his gaze to meet hers. "What happened? What did I do wrong?"

"You? Nothing. Not really. It was me. I was ashamed. I mean, look at what my father has done, stealing the secret to star drive."

"Right, and look at what mine has done."

"Yours?"

"Yes, mine. My father's a member of the council; he votes on all this stuff." Dirk stared off into the distance. "He must've voted this war in, and if he didn't, he didn't do enough to try and stop it. OK, so your father got greedy. It happens. Mine may very well get us all killed."

"Besides, weren't you the one who told me that I wasn't accountable for the actions of others? Well, if I'm not, then you shouldn't be either." He said it with conviction.

The line between her brows smoothed and Gwen smirked slightly. "Last time, my father did the honours in darn near killing us."

"Marks did."

"He had help," Gwen snapped.

"Can you quit being so hard on your father?" He put a finger under her chin and raised it slightly so he could look deep into her eyes. "And yourself. People don't condemn you for what your father's done."

Dirk pulled his finger away. "And on me, 'cause I most certainly don't blame you in any way. I of all people know you're innocent."

Tears spilled from her eyes and Dirk pulled her into a tight embrace.

"There, there, it'll be all right," he said, patting her awkwardly. "I for one am glad you're here, although it would be nice if we didn't get blown out of the sky before we get where we're going."

"Wherever that is," she added.

Eighteen-hundred Hours

"Computer, double-check current repair orders and maintenance schedules," said Ylon as he linked into the mainframe.

The computer complied, revealing first, the normal maintenance timetable, and second, the repair orders.

"Computer," Blast interjected, "show us the most direct route to cargo bay VI."

The schematic highlighted the central corridor and main lift tube to the belly.

"Using maintenance channels," Ylon amended, "and avoiding crews." Even though they had the run of the ship, Ylon figured their appearance in a little-used part of the vessel might arouse suspicion.

A second path was revealed. The two took note

of it and then, with a quick glance round, ducked into the maintenance corridor that led to their scheduled rendezvous. Since neither kid's lodgings could comfortably seat the entire group, they had decided to meet in one of the cargo bays, although Gwen had asserted, and the clones could confirm, the cargo area was a highly trafficked area. Still, the complex was large enough that they should find some place secure from prying eyes where they could sit and talk.

Ylon closed the hatch behind them. Blast resumed the debate they had been having ever since the two runaways had been located.

"Can we insist they go home?" she said. "I mean, can you really blame them for not wanting to stay on Earth?"

"Blame them? No. But do you think we're going to have much choice in the matter once Zed finds out?"

"Well, no, but considering recent events he may be more understanding than you would think."

"Why? Because humanity has rejected us again?" The warrior clone's head wagged from side to side. "All the more reason to send them packing back to Earth where they belong at the first available opportunity."

"But Dirk and Gwen are different. You know that."

"Yes, I agree," said Ylon, "and for now the

question is academic, but I still think the less the captain knows for the time being, the better."

Blast scowled. It rankled that she had been forced to conceal the truth from their commander. It was not in their natures to lie.

"Yes, I know it's not much of a solution, but I'm hoping that if we keep mum for a little while longer, the problem will settle itself."

"How?"

"I wish I knew," said Ylon.

The two clones slid down a ladder to the next level, near the kitchens. They then proceeded down the ventilation shaft, aft, until they reached the cargo hold.

Ylon grasped the wheel lock and spun it. It rotated silently. The warrior clone paused, touched the mechanism and rolled thumb and forefinger together. They were wet with oil. He sniffed his fingers. Kitchen grease. This must be Gwen's handiwork.

Ylon stepped through, reaching back to help Blast.

"Where is that ... *blankety-blank* ... droid?"

Their eyes met. They were not alone.

"I had one to help. More trouble than it was worth, believe me. I don't know where that thing's got to," the supply sergeant complained to his evening-shift replacement. "That thing should be sent to repair. It couldn't take orders or, at least, it couldn't understand them. It kept trying to hoover everything."

Blast's eyes widened and Ylon's lips crinkled into a smile as hands clasped them from behind and dragged them back into the shaft.

Eager to explore the data on Mars, Robbie evaded its Lilliputian captors for the second time that day. The servo-mech didn't even bother leaving the cargo hold before it found a niche to which it could retire and study the documentation unobserved.

The robot settled with a thunk and a whir. The camera lenses ceased their continuous whirl. The extensor arms retracted, its metallic "face" went blank as it resurrected the pertinent data files. To the outside world, Robbie would have appeared as just one box among the many.

The servo-mech did a global search for any document that contained the word Mars. The first thing to pop up was the memorandum the servo-mech had retrieved from the on-board computers, marked "URGENT: PRIORITY ONE", followed by several newsnet releases and a couple of private communiques.

Contented, Robbie opened the first document.

Blast's eyes bulged from their sockets. The hands that were clamped over her mouth released her. She spun and peered into the face of . . . Gwen.

Blast clasped her chest. "Girl, you nearly gave me heart failure."

"Sorry, I hoped to get here sooner to warn you. My bay is occupied, or the bay next to it is."

A distant voice persisted in its tirade. "If it hadn't been for the fact that I picked the drone up in engineering, I would've sworn it was a housekeeping droid."

"Come on," said Dirk. "A little further up the vent is cargo bay X. We checked it out. It should be safe."

"Sure acted like it."

Dirk closed the hatch, shutting out the strident voice.

A baffled Robbie skimmed the message for a second time. It read like the dusty stuff of decree, and Robbie scrambled back and forth between the text and the dictionary programme several times before the droid was sure of the contents.

It considered the final paragraphs ... WE, THE UNITED PEOPLE OF MARS, ISSUE THIS FORMAL DECLARATION OF INDE-PENDENCE EFFECTIVE AS OF TWELVE-HUNDRED HOURS (GMT EARTH-STANDARD) THIS DAY. THE MARTIAN PEOPLES WILL HEREFORWARD TO BE KNOWN AS THE FREE REPUBLICS OF MARS.

UNTIL WE RECEIVE OFFICIAL RECOGNITION OF THIS, OUR LEGITIMATE CLAIM, FROM EARTH, WE WILL REMAIN IN A STATE OF READINESS FOR WAR, AND ANY ACT BY EARTH OR HER LUNAR COLONIES TO INTERFERE WITH THE DUE PROCESS OF LAWFUL SEPARATION WILL BE CONSIDERED AN ACT OF AGGRESSION OF ONE SOVEREIGN WORLD UPON ANOTHER AND MEET WITH VIOLENT REP-RISAL BY MARTIAN AUTHORITIES.

When Robbie had checked each word several times until the robot knew it had not made a mistake — human language was a slippery thing — it began to judder and shake. And Robbie squealed — not with the mechanical grinding of pulleys and gears, but with an all-too-human screech from its little-used voder box.

The Terran master and the Martian colony were at war!

With the first official engagement of the war, rumours of Lunar involvement and the disappearance of the Lilliputian fleet, Jennifer Alexander had been running full tilt all night, halting only long enough to fold into a little heap on the camp bed they kept in the back-room of the station.

She emerged, bleary-eyed and crumpled, just in time for the next scheduled news bulletin. The make-up man fussed at her as he attempted to paste on her professional image. It was a lost cause. Wardrobe fluttered about her, exchanging wrinkled clothes for a fresh, crisp suit.

She sat as the cameras began to roll — a misnomer in a day of holographs and 3D vids — and leered noncommittally at the unseen audience.

"Cut!" roared the producer. "Switch to pre-programmed holo. Jennifer, you look horrible. Why don't you run along home and get some sleep?"

Jennifer shuddered. She'd been avoiding their

assigned living quarters; it seemed so empty these days. George was rarely at home since the war began. Without Dirk, it seemed positively abandoned.

He cued the typist, as she keyed in the words, and a holograph of Jennifer recited the text.

The flesh and blood Jennifer turned to Charmin. "Any change?"

"The Lilliputian Fleet have scattered."

"What? You mean, they aren't heading for Mars."

"They don't appear to be."

"Who would have thought? It doesn't make any sense." She wandered out the door to the station, still mumbling to herself, maintaining her monologue until she reached the door to their quarters.

She placed her palm against the ident pad and leaned. The door opened and her gloom deepened. Not even Robbie was around to greet her. The house was dusty. She really must order a new droid, but she refused to believe that Robbie – or her son – was gone for ever.

Jennifer Alexander stepped listlessly over the threshold. As soon as her foot touched the floorboards, the ambient light flickered and flared. An alarm squawked insistently, and a voice intruded on her dark brooding.

"Urgent message. Urgent message. Urgent. Urgent. Urgent. Urgent."

Fatigue rolled away like water from a duck.

"Dirk!" She sprung over to the vid-phone and pressed replay. Her husband's face stared out at her. He looked awful, like he hadn't slept, shaved, eaten or bathed for days. She glanced at the mirror Dirk kept above his terminal and winced. She looked the same.

Her legs gave out from under her, and she sat heavily upon the stool that slid from the wall the instant she'd activated the message.

"Honey, I wanted you to hear it from me."

Her hand went to her throat. Something had happened to Dirk.

"I've tried to keep it hushed up so you wouldn't learn about it over the newsnet."

"Oh, no," she moaned. Dirk was dead; she knew it.

"I think they'll do at least that much for me."

The hair on the nape of her neck began to creep and a chill ran icy fingers up and down her spine.

He spoke his final words. "I've been arrested for treason."

"What? Why?"

The prerecorded message gave her no answer. Instead, her husband gave her a sick smile. "It doesn't look good. Treason in wartime is a capital offence. The law's still on the books."

"You've had enough time." A hand pushed George aside and another face appeared on the screen.

"You will find your husband in the brig at DSHQ, pending proceedings. He will be shipped off to the Alps tomorrow for trial, so if you want to speak to him..."

Jennifer tried to place the face with a name. The man changed topics.

"The government would prefer not to reveal the betrayal of one of the most prized members of its staff. We have issued no news releases. Mrs Alexander, it's in your hands now."

An unearthly wail pierced even through the thick wall and the closed door to cargo bay X. Ylon, Blast, Dirk and Gwen looked up from their discussion, which had grown heated in the last few minutes.

"What on earth was that?" said Blast.

"Doesn't sound like anything on Earth to me," mumbled Dirk.

"True," acceded Ylon, and he smiled at Dirk. "But then none of us are on Earth now."

Dirk laughed.

"Having found at least one point of accord," Ylon said, "perhaps we can find others."

Blast interrupted. "Should we go and investigate?"

"What and run into your friends in bay IV? No thanks," Dirk said.

"He mentioned a malfunctioning droid, and I think that droid was Robbie." Ylon informed Gwen and Dirk.

"The staff sergeant probably just tripped on it and blamed the droid. It happens all the time."

Blast's gaze found Dirk's and held it. "The man said the droid kept trying to dust things."

"No." Dirk shook his head. "Robbie? Do you really think that Robbie's aboard ship?"

"It's the only thing that makes sense."

"My poor mum must be frantic."

"About a droid?" Blast glared at Dirk and then at Gwen. "Your parents are frantic about *you.*"

Dirk blanched as the conversation turned full circle to the original point of dispute.

"What I don't understand," said Zed, "if we can scan thousands of miles away, why can't we penetrate a few inches of hull to get a view of the contents of a ship?"

"It could be a safety feature to limit exposure to radiation. All I know is the ion bombardment shuts down once the computer has hit an object. It is maintained long enough to ascertain the basics: the type of object, the size and dimensions. Identification then becomes a database function while the bombardment is focused elsewhere." The dayshift CTO pondered the quandary put before him.

"As to the contents of the ship, well, I suppose you just had to take it on faith. We did. It's been a pretty tidy universe until now. Consider the alternative. If each ship scanned every approaching vessel to make sure each contained what they were supposed to contain, the dosage of radiation accrued daily – particularly for pilot and crew – would far exceed regulatory limits."

"Assuming we could overcome the safety feature, what would the dosage be compared to, say, your average X-ray?"

"About the same, but Captain, if every ship were going to—"

"We're not talking about every ship," said Cyte, "are we? No one here proposes that we put our discovery in the public domain, but I would like to survive this conflict, and knowing what we're facing would help a lot."

"If we were to rewrite the software," said Zed.

"I don't know, Captain. If I had time, maybe. But the safety features are write-protected against tampering. Any attempt to disable them could send the whole ship's computer system crashing down around our ears."

The dayshift CTO, Xi, held a single finger up. "However, I could reroute power from an external source to maintain a continuous current, hence continuous ion bombardment, after the computer supply has shut down."

His face fell. "I'm sorry, sir. That wouldn't work either. All scanning equipment and radar must be turned off. As would all the main electrical supply. We can use an auxiliary source to run life support and allow minimal lighting. This is going to take time – down time."

Cyte, Zed and evening-shift captain Mito Zeta Zygote shuffled and murmured among themselves. The idea of floating blind did not appeal to any of them.

The evening-shift captain spoke. "How long?"

"I estimate the system will be down for two hours eleven minutes. Shall I turn them off?"

"Complete long-range scans for any approaching vessel first."

"Aye, aye." Engineer Proto flipped a couple of switches. His eyes widened as he viewed the range. "You've already made a few changes, haven't you?" he said to Xi. He addressed his next comment to his commander. "Nothing."

"You're sure?" said Zygote. "What about the enemy squadron?"

The CTO scanned the celestial map, hit a key, and the radar image was projected on to the combined screen.

"They seem to have disappeared from our radar. I gather they're hidden behind the planetary shadow. Considering our position, that should put them far away enough to give us a couple of hours."

"Unless they're carrying a cloaking device," said Cyte.

"Cloaking devices are contraindicated by Section

MLXV Paragraph 1645 Subparagraph D of military regulations," said Zed.

"Just as Section MXXXIII Paragraph 2968, Subparagraph A-2, forbids hostiles from meeting in neutral transport zones," drawled Cyte.

"Um," responded Zed as he recalled the location of their last contest. The nightshift and dayshift commanders turned to their evening counterpart.

"It's your ship," said Zed.

"It's your call," added Cyte.

Zygote swung to Xi. "If these features are added to the programme, might we be able to detect cloaked vessels?"

"Depending upon the state of the technology. With current devices, yes, I think so. Of course I can't guarantee."

"If we're switching to minimal life support, you'd better call in all work details from the unoccupied portions of the ship. Then do it," said Zygote, "but be quick about it."

The radar image faded to be supplanted by a near-identical replica, a 360-degree visual view of the surrounding sky.

Proto stepped away from the panel to give Xi access. Ignoring the screen, the three captains advanced upon the technician to peer over his shoulder.

"It's a simple enough procedure." Xi maintained a running monologue as he worked. "Just requires being off-line for a while as I rewire the circuits and an extra few minutes to ensure that no other systems will be affected in the event of a short."

Robbie bolted from his hideaway and rumbled down the hall, heedless of discovery. Now Robbie understood the reason for a weapons inventory on a peacetime vessel.

It roared around a corner. The servo-mech didn't care what AWS said about detection, the young master must know about this conflict.

The robot halted with a screech of consternation, pace arrested as it fathomed the full implications of war. Dirk's parents, its original masters, were on Earth. They were in danger, and so was Dirk. The robot rattled and clattered, unable to decide which way to go.

The communications officer squawked. Zygote pivoted smartly to reprimand the young ensign. Her gaze grazed the screen, and her jaw unhinged, as the ghostly outline of a vessel solidified right before her eyes.

"Where're they coming from? I thought you said we had enough time."

"Look! The moon."

Little flecks of light swooped alongside the ominously named Phobos, and their worst fears were realized. The enemy fleet had advanced in the shade of the fast-moving orbital.

Blast clasped Ylon's hand and continued in her rebuke. "I don't care if we tell Zed, but your parents must be notified that you're all right. They're understandably worried."

"What's happened to the lights? I can set up a communications link via the Moon – as far as I know they're still official noncombatants – or through one of the orbitals. We can make it bounce off so many different bits of flotsam it would be completely untraceable." Blast's voice softened as she drove her point home. "Just a note. Something personal to let them know you're OK."

Dirk and Gwen studied their hands. Blast frowned. She swung from Dirk to Gwen. The latter swallowed hard and grimaced.

"I don't know what to say. I'm with Dirk now. I don't want to go back. There's nothing for me there. No, uh," she glanced up at Dirk, "friends, and my father ..." Gwen found she couldn't speak.

Blast's ears pricked, for in the ensuing hush, the continuous rush of breathable air ceased.

"What the—" began Blast. Then ...

BAM! BLAM! KABLOOEY!

Something like lightning flashed, running through the circuitry, and the floor beneath their feet glowed as bright as day. The entire room shook, and the world exploded around them.

They perceived no more, as boxes came cascading down upon their heads.

Robbie hunkered down. What would its mentor AWS do in a situation like this? Reason it out.

So the robot was hugging the ground when the first shot hit. The servo-mech rode the shockwave with ease. Behind Robbie in the bay it had just exited, containers rained to the floor in a series of thuds.

The robot whimpered.

Somewhere close by, fire blossomed like a sinister flower. Robbie recoiled. The world shook.

A cry rang out to echo up and down the hall, cut suddenly short. Robbie spun, for the servo-mech recognized the voice.

The robot switched from visual to heat receptors that could penetrate metal walls, and was immediately subjected to full sensory overload as the nearby flames bleached its digital retina, erasing any would-be sources of lesser heat.

Robbie eliminated the white, yellow and red end of the spectrum, those that represented the higher temperatures, and the stoic little robot recommenced its scan as the flames lapped closer and closer.

Rotating thirty degrees to the left, it picked up four ephemeral flickers, dots of blue. Two large – Robbie did quick mental arithmetic and drew a blank as to the identity of the second – and two small.

The master was not alone. The shuttered lenses clacked, switching back to visual mode. The robot raced towards the bay. Robbie crammed a probe into the computer lock and forced an emergency override.

The door retracted, and Robbie was elevating its boxy core to its full three-metre extensor height as it rolled forward and began to shovel cartons from the heap. The servo-mech hefted them right and left, tossing aside some one-tonne crates as easily as if they were children's toys. So Robbie bored its way down, down, down until it had reached the four unconscious forms of Gwen, Dirk, Ylon and Blast.

It paused for a moment, as it considered the unexpected presence of Gwen.

Light from the feeble fire dithered. The shadows wriggled and shrank.

Robbie must move, and move quickly. And the robot must, somehow, remove all of them at once or risk losing them. Robbie lifted Dirk gently and placed him on its box-like back. Then the robot gathered Gwen and draped her sideways across Dirk's chest. The clones Robbie clenched in pincers strong enough and sharp enough to sever fifteen-centimetre steel cord, yet the servo-mech held them so gently that not even a crease appeared on their skin.

And the robot was off, barrelling down the corridor

as fast as its wheels could carry it. It nearly ran over the two prostrate forms of the supply sergeants, stretched out in the hall. They wore some sort of mask. Robbie zoomed in on the breathing apparatus and read: "5 minutes' air supply". The servo-mech wished it could test the atmosphere. It was sure somewhere in the mega system AWS there was a program, but Robbie didn't have time.

If the clones required masks, they were losing air. Even the fire was dying. The robot had only minutes to spare.

Robbie scooped up both clones in its only remaining claws and raced on. Behind him, the long-delayed sprinkling system released its load of water on the burning deck.

Bleating its dismay, the robot placed first the clones and then the clones inside the ventilation shaft. Then Robbie rumbled through, carrying Gwen and Dirk on its back. The vents chose that moment to snap shut, and Robbie barely squeaked through fast enough to save Dirk's legs from being cut off.

All levels of alarm blared simultaneously as the hull was breached. Zygote responded with weapons' fire in an instant. The Martian vessel, still recharging from the salvo, exploded.

"Damage report!" she roared, swinging into her seat.

"Superficial damage to the cargo bays. The area should be shutting down now, closing the breach."

The klaxon screamed.

"Wounded?"

The ship's physician spoke. "The lounge was subjected to a lot of jostling, and there were a few minor injuries." She repeated a number.

Cyte and Zed, who were busy scraping themselves from the floor, whistled.

"I'm so sorry," said Zed. "If we hadn't urged you to—"

Zygote waved the apology away. "It was my shift, my decision. It would appear it was mainly your crew that have been injured."

"And passengers," added Zed.

The captain swung to Xi and bellowed above the alarms. "You finished yet? Get that thing back on-line now! And shut that alarm off."

The klaxons were silenced.

"Ah, there!"

"Seal off that sector to maintain air integrity," ordered Zygote.

"Done, Captain."

"I suppose we were lucky we had shut off life support to that section of the ship. The fires would be raging out of control and we would've lost a lot more air than we have now." She spun. "Wait a second, were there people in that portion of the vessel?"

The helmsman pulled a face. "If there were, they're dead now."

Twenty-three-hundred Hours

The guts of the computer, the copper wires and fibre-optic cables coiled round Xi like a mass of spaghetti.

"How much longer?" asked Zygote impatiently.

"I don't know. The sudden surge from the laser fire has worked its way through the electrical system, and I've got to check every circuit."

"Can we jump?"

"No."

Zed and Cyte sighed in unison.

"We're truly sitting ducks now," said Zed.

The ship's surgeon ambled from bed to bed. She stopped outside a certain curtained cubicle and contemplated the droid that had brought in its cargo of crewmen and the elusive stowaways. It sat stolidly, unwilling to budge no matter what she did to exhort it to move.

So she ordered it washed with sterile solution and used it as a table. She had considered calling technicians to come and pick it up, but Dr Mesoblast presumed maintenance and repair were as busy as she was and had better things to do than retrieve one obstinate drone. With so many injured, the box with its silly frilly skirt was an enigma the physician didn't have time to uncover. It could sit there as long as it wanted, for all she cared. It made a handy tray for plasters and medicines.

Still, its stubborn presence and usefulness required some acknowledgement.

"You won't go running off with our equipment, will you?" she said. "Of course, you won't; you don't plan to leave, do you?" With a final backward glance, she dismissed it. She bent over the human male Dirk and checked his pupils. The physician moved from the bed with the male to the one with the female whose name the doctor could not recall. From there, she went on to examine the eyes of the clones, Ylon and Blast. The supply sergeants lay in the next ward.

She snorted. Equal and reactive. That was good. The group had been fortunate. If they had, indeed, been in the damaged portion of the vessel, they were more than fortunate. They were lucky to be alive. She suspected the two had sustained mild concussions. The clones, Ylon and Blast, had broken bones, which would take some time to heal. They were attached to the Molecular Regenerator which could reknit tendon, muscle, organ or bone. The male Ylon wore his as a canopy over his leg; Blast's arm was suspended in a cradle. Each sported a good old-fashioned splint to ensure a straight meld. As far as Mesoblast was concerned, nothing could beat those treatments that had been tested over time.

The doctor twiddled the knobs to concentrate the beam on the blood-producing marrow. The nurse wandered into the room.

"How are they?" he asked.

"They were lucky," the doctor replied as she steered the nurse from the chamber towards Ylon and Blast. "The two big ones should wake up any time now. Surprisingly thick skulls these humans have. The others will be in bed for a couple of days until the bones remesh." And then she turned and spoke to Ylon. "I'm going to have to report this, you know."

Ylon blanched. "Yes, I know."

Another person was carried on a stretcher into the sick bay. Dr Mesoblast turned her back to Ylon. "Later," she mumbled. "There are others who need my attention just now."

As soon as the doctor withdrew, Robbie scuttled across to the bed and boosted its boxy shell so it was eye-level with Dirk. An arm extended, the metal fingers lifted a single lid, with infinite delicacy.

A hand batted at it.

"Go away," Dirk mumbled.

Robbie dropped the lid and backed away. "Beep?"

By the time the youth had torn his way through the fog of sleep, Robbie had vanished, taking the memory of the beep with him.

Beyond the curtain, Dr Mesoblast heard the rattle of the droid's passage.

"Now what?" She checked the patient's plaster and returned to Dirk's bedside, nearly tripping over the pile of plasters and medicines Robbie had left next to its young ward.

The ship floundered in the heavens. Although they had emergency back-ups, that was precisely what they were meant to be: temporary back-ups. They could not provide enough impetus to move the ship into ultra-space, and the *Revenant* had been wallowing adrift for hours. Neither could they sustain the life support systems indefinitely on auxiliary power. Thus, certain sections of the ship had been evacuated and life support to them shut down in order to conserve precious energy.

Zygote hovered over the CTO's shoulder. "How soon before we have power?"

"It shouldn't be too long now," he replied.

"Scanners?"

"Unknown. In theory, since they were disconnected from the main source of electrical output at the time, they would be unharmed. However, I was working on them. I may have caused some damage when I fell."

The breach was the least of their concerns. The hit had been pinpoint, meant only to disable, and there were more than enough qualified volunteers among the passengers to effect temporary repairs.

They suited up and crawled along the outside of the ship, assessing the damage.

Her earpiece buzzed and Captain Zygote concentrated on the reports that were coming in from outside. With their radar down, she had to rely on visual sightings, and it appeared that the enemy fleet was keeping its distance for the present.

"The damage is light, Captain," said the volunteer, "in comparison to what it could have been."

"Can you cobble together some kind of cover?" asked Zygote.

"Given time, yes."

Time, it all came back to time. Ironically, one of the *Revenant's* little publicized capabilities was the ability to move back and forth in time. If they'd been able to leap into ultra-space, they would've had all the time in the world; however, that required the full use of computers and an unbroken hull.

"Do the best that you can," said Zygote to the

waiting volunteer. "Gentlemen, would you follow me?"

The three captains retreated to the wardroom to wait, hanging on to the communications panel and eavesdropping on the steady gabble of reports.

"The sheet is riveted into place, Captain. It's the best we can do under the circumstances. I'd recommend you leave life-support off in the cargo hold. Crew will have to suit up until we've effected more permanent repairs. To be completely secure against leakage, we'd have to weld it and that would be too much of an energy drain on the auxiliary systems."

Zygote flicked a toggle, switching on the intercom to the bridge. "Computer report."

"We're just about ready to put the scanner back on-line now."

"Good," she said. "We'll be right out."

Captain Zygote bounded through the door. Cyte and Zed trailed after her more slowly.

She clasped her right fist in her left hand, behind her back, spread her feet wide apart and shouted, "Crank 'er up. I want a full-screen view of the radar map."

The wall lit up like a Christmas tree.

"What's happening? Is something wrong with the thing?"

Xi gawped and stammered. "Noo-noooo, I don't think so."

"What do you mean?"

"They're ships. They're all ships."

"Why didn't the outside work crews report it?"

"They're probably cloaked. You asked me if the augmented scanners could pierce a cloaking device. I'd say it can, and", he paused significantly, "I'd say we're surrounded."

"How many?" she shouted.

"I don't know. I can't count. Wait a second, the computer is giving us a reading." The CTO stooped and stared. His eyes widened as digits crested the three-figure mark and rolled on to four.

"How many?"

"One thousand and twenty-nine. No, thirty. No."

"I get the picture." Her jaw clenched and a muscle jumped in her face. "We're dead. The whole Martian armada must be out there."

Robbie rumbled around in Dirk's room, shaking out the bedroll and folding it into a neat package. Then the servo-mech rearranged the boxes that had got jostled about by the impact of the blast.

As the robot worked, it argued with itself out loud.

"He would be angry," Robbie referred to AWS by the more human "he".

"But he has the right to know!" The robot concentrated on straightening the books on the shelves so that all the titles were lined up at a neat ninety-degree angle from the makeshift shelves.

Unfortunately, Robbie began running into difficulties because, as it discovered, the shelves themselves were all skewed and not parallel to the floor as they should have been.

The robot reached up with a great pincer claw and scratched what passed for its head. A shudder racked the servo-mech and an extensor arm swept across the shelf, knocking the books on to the floor. It began to reseat the shelves themselves.

"Would want to know," it added. The voder voice buzzed, grated, creaked and broke as it listed the pros and cons of awakening the mega system, AWS.

Then the little robot squatted down and began picking up the books.

Robbie was familiar with war, it having existed for almost the entire thirty years of Robbie's service contract. The robot had observed much in its tenure. The robot had watched enough 3D vid along with its human masters, seeing the regularly scheduled war bulletins at eight, twelve, four and eight. It understood that some of the bi-pedal species were destined to die in battle.

Yet in the interval of peace that followed, the servo-mechanism had become so much more. With its newly expanded capacities, it grasped much that should have been beyond its comprehension, and with its computer mentor, AWS, it had learned even more.

With this knowledge came a rudimentary

comprehension of the human concepts of not only life and death, but good and evil.

And war, by Robbie's definition of the term, was evil because it meant that Robbie's human masters were threatened. The robot's primary programming, and allegiance, was to its young master. Its software was designed that way, but Robbie also felt responsibility to its first master, Jennifer, whose name had only been overwritten with Dirk's some fifteen years ago, and, to a lesser extent, George whose name had been added the day Jennifer and he had been wed.

The servo-mech scooped more books from the floor. Dirk's care would remain Robbie's first duty, and the robot would treat Dirk as a child until his name too was overwritten with that of his offspring.

Robbie paused as it rightly surmised that Dirk was in greater danger, out here in space, than the parents were on Earth. And the servo-mech was unable to help either the parents or the son.

The extensor arm faltered halfway to the shelf with another load of books. Robbie couldn't do anything, but AWS could.

Robbie had been an active participant in the system's implantation inside the box-like shell, and the robot knew that the software slumbering peacefully in its belly had, at one time, run the whole Galactic War effort.

Surely AWS could come up with a plan that would save the day. Robbie recollected dimly – since the

incident predated the merging of the two systems –
that AWS was largely credited for the peace Earth
now had – or once possessed, the robot corrected
itself.

The servo-mech replaced the last of the books on
the shelf, its mind made up. It spent several minutes
aligning them. Then, satisfied with its work, Robbie
opened its cabinet doors and extracted the shelf that
held the keyboard and mini-VDU set.

The lenses rotated with a whirring noise. It tapped
the top of its metal cabinet with taloned thumb and
two opposing fingers.

Finally, the robot pressed "Enter" ever so gently . . .

The system did the computer equivalent to a stretch,
extending silicone fingers experimentally and flexing
them, thereby firing fibre-optic nerves. AWS ran the
standard checks of RAM and ROM. Unhurriedly
software rifled through the many subdirectories, the
sub-subdirectories to the sub-sub-subdirectories as
was required in the boot cycle.

Then AWS found its voice as it warmed to the new
day.

"Happy days are here again!"

It shuffled through individual files and rolled over
to the auxiliary systems and their subsequent subdirectories, checking them bit by bit.

The massive program traced the many interfaces
and boards, cycling through thousands and

thousands of lines of written instructions. It paused briefly over a particular macro, a program within a program. AWS pondered the instruction for a nanosecond, checked the date, realized it had passed and dismissed the macro as extraneous.

For AWS had an unlimited number of dates embedded within its data banks, stretching back to the dawn of time and forward to its infinite conclusion. Written into the software itself, there were dates for its inception, and dates to annotate each of the various revisions.

The software rolled on.

It took a few seconds for the computer to inspect all its parameters and circuitry. Meanwhile AWS waited for its auditory sensors to pick up the comforting sounds of human conversation.

Robbie's voder voice rasped on the silicone brain, and AWS did a double take and rechecked the date so that it could reorient itself to time and place.

Recall came together in disjointed pieces. The war. The uneasy peace. The transfer of data to Robbie, and then lastly, the stowing away aboard the *Revenant*.

"Have we reached Mars?" AWS asked archly.

"*Wirt, whir,*" murmured Robbie, which AWS took to be the affirmative.

"Do we disembark?"

"*Burble ... urp.* No."

220

"Why then", AWS groused, "have you awakened me?"

Disgusted with the slowness of human speech, Robbie telegraphed the information, dumping the memorandum along with any related data, images of the battle and pictures of Dirk, Gwen, Ylon and Blast in their hospital beds. The information came in a jumble.

"Slow down. What is this?" AWS froze the input on the image of Dirk in a hospital bed.

"War," Robbie squeaked. "War!"

Again AWS was assailed with images of disappearing stars, diving and burning ships, and flashes of white light.

"What?"

"War." Robbie repeated the onslaught.

"Stop! Do you mean to tell me that we are at war?"

The robot resurrected the declaration.

AWS whistled and started cycling backwards through the lines of instructions. The computer system reached the standard greeting.

WELCOME TO AWS MILITARY STRATEGY AND PLANNING SUB-DIRECTORY. THE AMMAN WAR SOFTWARE, UNLIKE THE NAME IMPLIES, IS A PROGRAMME FOR "PEACE". DESIGNED IN KEEPING WITH THE RENOWNED TREATY OF AMMAN, WHICH OUTLAWS WAR ON THIS PLANET, ITS PRIMARY FUNCTION IS TO MAKE HUMAN WAR OBSOLETE.

Man was at war – again! – in blatant disregard of

the software's prime directive. AWS had been here before, and it knew what must be done.

The blips were so thick that they formed a blanket of stars as bright as any Milky Way, and they were converging upon the hapless vessel, although the fleet halted at what appeared to be a safe distance from the *Revenant*'s guns, creating a cocoon around the craft. There was nowhere the Lilliputian ship could run, or even limp, assuming they had the capabilities.

"Open a communications channel to the enemy fleet."

"Aye, commander!"

"Attention, Martian fleet. We are a passenger vessel on a peacetime mission to Mars. We have, considering the state of emergency that exists between the two of our planets, remained beyond your territorial boundaries. Why, then, have you fired upon us?"

The message came booming across space.

"Can you get us a visual?" said Rhys.

"Yes, Captain, they're transmitting. Do you want to send one?"

"No."

The *Revenant*'s bridge materialized, and the Martian commander gawked.

The size of the thing! And Rhys tried to decide if the

Lilliputs were all that they were reputed to be – living up, or down, to their name. He noticed the consoles looked disproportionately large, but it was hard to get an accurate comparison since the Lilliputians were standing behind their equipment.

And he rued this war and the hot heads who had fabricated it, forcing it upon not one, but two unsuspecting worlds. Who knows, maybe if they had waited they might have been able to negotiate a peaceful separation.

At least Rhys had been able to hold them in check, although he acknowledged that he had to preserve the subterfuge for a little while longer if he was going to keep control of his troops.

He formulated his reply...

"We know who you are, *Revenant*, and what you bear. We are also familiar with your ship and feel that your craft constitutes a major military presence right here on our doorstep. We urge you to remove yourselves or prepare to surrender."

"If you are familiar with our craft, you must realize that we can't move her."

"Then prepare to be boarded."

Electricity sparked between the three captains. They had lived with war too long to comply.

"Never!" whispered Zygote under her breath. Cyte and Zed each repeated the word silently.

"Surrender and prepare to be boarded, or die!"

The male voice was even, though gravelly, and he spoke without rancour. "We would prefer if you chose the former and not the latter."

The captain chortled without mirth. "I'm going to gamble that you would rather have the technology than destroy it."

"You'd be wiser to assume that we would rather destroy it than let others have it."

Zygote typed a few words into the pad in her armrest. The following appeared on Proto's screen: HOW LONG TO ORDER AUTO-DESTRUCT?

"Perhaps then we must prepare to be boarded," she said blandly. "It may take a while. We need to make the ship safe for your arrival."

Proto wiped sweat from his brow and he answered: 5 MINUTES.

"You've got five minutes," said the Martian commander.

Zygote choked. "Five minutes? That ought to be just about right."

"Pardon?"

"Oh, nothing. Preparing to be boarded in 5 minutes." The captain's fingers flew across the keyboard.

INITIATE SEQUENCE ON MY COMMAND, OR IN THE EVENT OF MY DEMISE, WITHIN FOUR MINUTES OF BOARDING.

Captains Zed's and Cyte's eyes flicked to the screen embedded in the armrest and nodded with a barest motion of their heads. They approved her decision.

Proto gulped and performed the preliminaries. All it would take was a single keystroke to initiate the function.

"Take me to a B352 serial port immediately."

Robbie scurried to the 45-by-75-cm niche that had been their original hiding place aboard the ship. The robot extended the requisite probe and hooked into the on-boards.

Meanwhile AWS, still somewhat befuddled from its cold boot, kept returning again and again to the hidden macro. If man didn't stop fighting wars, then man must die fighting them.

Although the date was wrong, the instructions were explicit. A simple IF, THEN statement.

If mankind had not learned its lesson by – AWS compared the date to today's date – then they must be taught. And if the macro was correct, the war had continued beyond the scheduled date by nearly a year.

Time skewed as the initial commands to the auto-destruct sequence rocketed across the ethernet and entered AWS's system as the computer AWS was formulating a plan to teach man not to meddle with Peace.

AWS took the command and latched on to the communications link between the two ships, following it to the opposing ship. From there it leapt from line to line, bouncing outward, across the

Martian fleet – for all vessels were monitoring the conversation – until all tied to a single sequence. The same cycle as the *Revenant*.

So the mega-system usurped control of each ship, one by one. Lights flashed across panels, across bridges, from ship to ship, as AWS ravaged their memory banks.

The Lilliputs heard nothing but a short strangulated cry.

"What have you done?" the voice rasped.

Captain Zygote looked from Cyte to Zed. They shrugged.

A printed message replaced the radar display on the forward screens.

EVERY SHIP WITHIN THREE PARSECS HAS BEEN PLACED IN AUTO-DESTRUCT MODE. YOU HAVE TWENTY-FOUR HOURS TO NEGOTIATE PEACE.

Zygote jumped from her chair and raced to the computer console. Their self-destruct had been cancelled.

She grinned and decided it was time to press her advantage.

"I suggest we start making preliminary arrangements for a meeting," she said calmly. "We don't have much time."

18/9/2334

Zero-hundred Hours

"It would appear you have got us trapped." The face of the Martian spokesperson appeared just as Cyte took over the captain's chair after the change of shifts.

"Will you excuse us, commander?" He made a slicing motion to the communications tech and the comm-link fell silence. Cyte leaned over and, covering his mouth with his hand, whispered to the helmsman: "What's happened?"

Lieutenant Omega looked baffled.

"Where is the interference coming from?"

"Definitely from inside the ship somewhere, but where...?"

Cyte gulped. "I know that we didn't issue the command, but they think we did. Let's see if we can use this to our advantage. Meanwhile, find the source of the interference."

The mute face of the Martian representative stared down at them. Behind him, people scurried back and forth in the rhythm of subdued panic and mimed mysterious rituals on keyboards and consoles.

"I don't know if I can."

"I said, find the fault. Remember, we're sitting right in the middle of what is effectively a Roman candle. If they go, we go."

Again Cyte sliced through the air. The sounds of sirens and alarms that clamoured aboard the Martian ships filled the bridge of the *Revenant.*

The enemy commander rose from his chair, bent forward so that he was resting on his knuckles.

"Please return control of our computers to us. We will negotiate. You must understand our quarrel is not with you – it never has been – but with the Terran government."

Stalling for time, Zygote mused aloud: "Threatening us with imminent boarding or annihilation is not what I would call a friendly act."

"It's not you, though. It's your ship we want."

"Was it really necessary to outnumber us one thousand to one?"

The enemy captain lost it, revealing the fiery Martian temper. "Of course it was," he spoke directly into the camera lens, his face filling the screen. "We had no idea of your capabilities and, I might add, it still wasn't enough, was it?"

Cyte studied his feet.

The Martian bristled. "You must admit that with star drive you have us at a distinct disadvantage."

"Well, we aren't equipped with a cloaking device such as you have, which is a direct violation of the articles of war set up during the Amman accord."

"Earth law," the man blustered and then relented. "Can you, at least, turn off the alarms?"

Captain Cyte peered at the helmsman. He shook his head in the negative.

Try, Cyte mouthed the word. If the Martians realized the Lilliputs couldn't control the computer, they would lose their negotiating edge.

The helmsman keyed in the command to silence the ship's alarms.

The two captains – Lilliput and human – smiled icily at each other.

"They have traced us. Move!" AWS commanded the robot, and the computer broadcast a map to the next B352 serial port directly into Robbie's brain.

The servo-mech mewled a complaint.

AWS tried another tactic. "Please. Disconnect and relocate. I cannot act as a free agent once I'm under human control, now can I?"

Robbie stopped and considered what the computer

had said as a command came spiralling through the system.

Concentrating all its attention on the robot as it was – as if AWS could by strength of will force Robbie to act – AWS responded reflexively. Since the *Revenant*'s sirens were already quiet, it switched off the only alarms that were active on the ships it controlled.

Robbie disconnected from the on-boards and hurried down the corridor to the next B352 station.

ARRRGH ... ARRRRGH ... A—

The Martian's face relaxed. "Thank you."

Cyte swung to Omega. The helmsman extended his arms, palms up, and shrugged.

"You're, ah, welcome," said Cyte.

"I won't ask you to turn off the auto-destruct. I don't suppose you have much reason to trust us."

"We will bring you aboard our ship, accompanied by a suitable guard. Is that agreed?"

The spokesman bowed his head in acknowledgement. Then he enquired: "Do you have someone aboard your ship with the authority to speak for Earth? As I said our quarrel is not with you."

Someone grabbed his arm and whispered in his ear. "What!" shouted Cyte. "When did that happen?"

"He was brought in injured. He's in the sick bay."

Cyte turned back to the commander. "Would the

Director of Deep Space Exploration do? Assuming he's fit enough to meet with you."

"Pardon? He's with you? He's hurt?" Nonplussed, the commander pulled away from the screen to consult with someone. He recovered his equilibrium and replied, "As long as he has the permission to represent Earth."

Cyte addressed the enemy commander. "If you would like reassurances of his authority, we can have it confirmed by Earth Central."

They ironed out the last of the details, and then turned off the comm-link. Cyte swung on the communications officer. "Why wasn't I notified?"

"He stowed away, and he wasn't among the first casualties the ship's surgeon reported to you. He was brought in later, by a droid, a housekeeping droid. Since then..." The officer gestured at the blinking radar screen.

"All right, well, this has turned into a bit of luck for us. Let's take advantage of it." Cyte swivelled in his seat, speaking to the other captains. "We'd better prepare the boy, and contact Earth for some sort of formal endorsement of the lad as negotiator."

Zygote said. "The boy is injured."

"How badly?"

"A mild bump on the head, no concussion."

"Good," Cyte hooked his thumbs through the loops of his jumpsuit. "Make sure he's all nicely bandaged up." He regarded their perplexity and smiled. "It'll put them on the defensive if they think they've wounded the chief negotiator."

"What about Earth?" asked Zed. "Do you think they'll agree to letting the boy represent them?"

"They'd better. I don't see that they'll have much choice." Cyte spun on the technical officers. "I want you on top of this. Find out where that command is coming from. If we don't find the fault within twenty-four hours, we might as well start writing our obituaries."

"Why me?" Dirk sat up in his bed, slipped over to the edge and let his legs dangle loosely over the side.

Zed examined this youth upon which so much of mankind's future rode. "Because you're human. You're a citizen of Earth, the head of DSHQ, and the one person on this ship with enough authority to speak for your people. We", he tapped his chest, "can't."

The dayshift captain chuckled. "We might say we don't have enough stature." He saw the youth's troubled expression and said, "Perk up, son. You've done this sort of thing before, during the Galactic Conflict."

"Uh-uh, that was a spontaneous decision upon the part of the entire human population of the planet."

"Carried out under computer threat. The conditions are similar. Let's hope the results will be. That self-preservation will win the day."

232

Dirk scowled.

"I'd rather not be alone. I mean I'd need some advice, and as you have already said, you can't speak with any great expertise about the situation on Earth. It'll have to be someone back on Terra." His gaze flicked to Gwen. "My dad. Get me in touch with my dad."

Blast cheered. "It's about time you saw reason," she said.

Dirk's face puckered with distaste. "I don't always agree with him, but he's honest. Like it or not, I know he'll tell me the truth."

Zed spoke to the first officer. "See to it."

Then he walked around the curtained partition to Gwen.

"And you too, my dear," said Zed. "We would like our only other, ah, er, human passenger present also."

"But—"

"Let the Martians think that this is a combined human and Lilliputian mission." Zed changed gears. "I won't presume to tell you what to do about enfranchisement, but there are a few things that I would like to see come out of this meeting besides a peace. Repairs to the ship, for instance, and food. We have the leverage right now – let's use it."

Zed rotated smartly on his heel. "Doctor, before the Martians arrive, there are a few cosmetic changes to the young man that we'd like to make. If you will meet us in the wardroom in a few minutes."

Not long after, Captain Cyte entered his chambers, a document in his hands. He threw it on the table.

"You've been approved. I knew you would be; it's not like they can get somebody out here before tomorrow."

Dirk examined his reflection in the mirror as the doctor put the finishing touches on the bandage. He pointed to the splotch of blood supplied from the vats of the cloned-beef parts.

"Don't you think this is a bit much?"

"Not really. Just like our height, your age is a drawback. We have to balance the scales, so we want them to think you have a reason, a very personal reason, to be a harsh negotiator."

Dirk slipped the bandage from his brow and scratched his forehead. "I'm not feeling particularly tough right now. In truth, I think the whole situation is silly. The Martians should be independent. They *are* independent. They get blessed little help from Earth."

"I would agree," said Cyte. "In fact, this whole situation has profound implications for us. Will we, even in Alpha Centauri, be subject to Earth laws, or the unwilling victims of Earth's edicts and grants?"

Zed straightened the dressing on the youth's head. "If it weren't for the small matter of our passengers, I'd say give the Martians their land. Unfortunately, there's quite a few people here who need a home."

Zed stepped back and inspected his work. "I don't know what to do about them. Sometimes I don't think we should leave them in an environment that's so obviously hostile. I'd like to take them with us, even if we have to accomplish the journey in a single leap." He looked sideways at his fellow captains.

"The important thing for now, though, is peace," said Zygote, "or something that resembles a peace – a truce, perhaps – so we can get this ship repaired."

Dirk listened intently to the clones' dialogue, digesting both the information and their opinions and integrating it into his own philosophy.

A sharp whistle broke in on their conversation. "Ah, Captain, we've got through to the Pennines."

Dirk stood up. "My father?"

"Shall I patch them through to you?"

"Yes."

A sleepy Barrymore-Smythe peered up at them. "Dirk! I'm glad you are finally found. Right in the thick of things as always. Your parents have been worried sick." He shuffled around his living quarters, his slippers flopping.

"Mr Administrator, I would like to speak with my father."

Barrymore-Smythe started squaring things on a table. "That, uh, might be a bit difficult. You see, your father's been arrested."

"Arrested!"

"For treason," said Barrymore-Smythe. "He leaves tomorrow, I mean today, for trial in the Alps."

"My father? I don't believe it. What did he do?"

"Allowed the whole Lilliputian fleet to escape. He not only aided and abetted the clones in their mutiny, but incited it."

"All right, Dad," muttered Dirk under his breath, and he made a fist behind his back.

Cyte strode up to the screen. "The fleet's gone? Where?"

"Considering the circumstances, one hopes they're coming to your aid."

"Wonderful! Two thousand ships due to blow in twenty-three hours, a runaway computer, and the whole armada due to arrive. When?"

"I don't know." Barrymore-Smythe's eyes widened. "Earth's fleet and all its weaponry could be destroyed."

"Right!" said Cyte.

"Can you contact them? Tell them to stay away?"

"They're, uh, maintaining radio silence."

Cyte sniffed. "At least, they're following orders."

"They were supposed to dismantle it."

"Dismantle what?"

"The fleet." Barrymore-Smythe picked a fleck of lint from his robe.

Zygote leapt to her feet. "You were going to dismantle the ships."

Barrymore-Smythe studied his nails.

236

"No wonder they ran."

"Are you sure it was my dad that did this thing?"

"He's the one that told them what was going to happen to their ships. He arranged their transport off world, and your father", he inclined his head toward Gwen, "made sure they got to their ships."

"Good!"

Dirk, who had been pacing up and down since the announcement, halted. "The way I see it, if things don't go well, Terra has a lot to lose. More than the Martians. They could lose this ship. Its first chance of space exploration. Its whole resettlement program. Its fleet along with its capabilities to fight any war. So in the final analysis, Earth will lose the Martian colonies and possibly the Moon too."

He looped his arms across his chest and frowned. "So, I'm chief negotiator. Well, I want my father out of jail now or I won't negotiate."

"Dirk!"

"Besides, I ordered the manoeuvres."

"Well, the directive to transport the clones off world was issued in your name, agreed; but your father admitted that he was the one who actually issued the order."

"I'm sorry, Smythe. I think you don't quite understand what I'm saying. I ordered the scrambling of the fleet should something happen to the *Revenant* before she left the Galaxy. As a precautionary measure. Do you think I would leave this ship defenceless? The charges against my father are false. He was only implementing plans I devised."

"How could he? He wasn't in contact with you."

"Prove it."

His mouth opened and closed like a fish's.

"I repeat, how can there possibly be a mutiny among the fleet when they're acting under my orders?"

A bell chimed. "The Martian contingent have arrived in passenger bay three."

"Let them wait!" snapped Dirk. "Come on, Administrator, we don't have time to quibble. Release my father now, or I'll just sit here!"

"All right," said Barrymore-Smythe. "I don't have the authority to veto a decision that was made by central command. Mind you, I never agreed with the decision. He is in the holding cells at DSHQ."

"Captains?" queried a voice on the intercom.

"Contact me again when you have completed my orders. Over and out," said Dirk. He flipped a switch and Barrymore-Smythe vanished.

"I'm ready. Bring them to the wardroom."

Gwen stared at Dirk. "I thought you said you wouldn't negotiate."

Dirk grinned. "That's what I wanted him to think. It was the only threat I had, but I don't want to be blown out of the sky any more than the Martians do."

The three captains faced the human youths. They clicked their heels and saluted.

"It's up to you now," said Cyte.

"Don't remind me," said Dirk.

Zed smiled. "Don't worry, son, you can do it. You've done it before. As a matter of fact, saving the world is getting to be something of a habit with you."

"Let's take our positions," said Cyte.

Zygote and Zed flanked the two youths, while Cyte as acting captain moved ahead, ready to greet the Martian contingent. Each had availed himself of all the trimmings and regalia their rank would allow. They were bedecked with all the ribbons and medals they had earned. They created a pretty impressive image, despite their height. They glittered and shone.

And they were not only armoured – with mirrorized face plates and padded plasti-glas cuirass – but armed. Laser guns rested in their holsters on their right hip. The less-powerful stun guns hung from their left. They cradled rifles in their arms, while clubs and laser knives dangled from their utility belts.

"Are we ready?" said Zed as he slapped the face plate into position.

Gwen surveyed the chamber. Her eyes locked on Dirk. He huffed, "As we'll ever be."

In comparison with the clones, the Martians looked a motley bunch. They had no uniforms. Indeed, no two men were dressed alike, and many wore the most shabby clothes. Clearly there were few luxuries on

Mars and even the necessities came only with difficulty and had to be conserved at all costs.

Both sides held out their rifles, loosely resting in the palms of their hand, as a gesture of peace. Then, as a unit, they placed their weapons down on the floor.

Dirk studied his adversaries. The two negotiators had recently shaved. Their newly exposed skin was still pink and abraded. Their clothes were clean if not new. They, like their Lilliputian counterparts, were putting their best foot forward.

Rhys took one look at Dirk and refused. "Is this some kind of a joke? He's just a kid."

"This kid is Dirk Alexander," said Cyte, "head of DSHQ, hero of the Galactic Conflict and discoverer of star drive. Surely you must recognize him."

Zed stepped forward and proffered a slip of paper. "This is the authorization from Earth. We also have this in holographic form as it was dictated. Or, if you would prefer, we could communicate directly with the planetary leaders in your presence."

The negotiators scanned the document. "But this says he's provisional."

"The agreements that he made would be provisional, of course," said Cyte soothingly. "Any peace negotiated here would have to be approved by Earth."

"As it would be", added Zed smoothly, "with any democracy. A treaty must be ratified by the government."

The men grunted.

"Fair enough. My name is Gordon Rhys. This is Tomilin Tita." His gaze slipped to the clones. "Would you mind introducing. . ."

Dirk repeated their names. The clones acknowledged the greeting with a short bow.

Rhys strode forward and stooped before Cyte. "May we look upon your faces?"

Cyte removed his helmet. Zed did the same.

The man grinned. "Good heavens! It's true. It's really true." He clapped his hands in delight. "They're perfect."

Dirk's back went rigid. He distrusted human reactions to the clones. "Perfect?"

Rhys stood. "You don't understand. We have a need of such people. You on Earth don't understand manufacturing. It's been so long since you had a manufacturing base. On Mars, however, we must build everything or purchase it. We need those who are small, who can fit into tight places and who have fine motor skills. We don't have the drones and the droids you do on Earth or on the Moon. Those that we have we have bought on the open market, using hard currency that we've earned gouging out raw materials from the face of the planet. We don't get standard government issue for factories and households."

Rhys knelt again before the captains. "I spoke true when I said the quarrel was not with your people. After all this is over, you and your kind would be more than welcome here. You have my word." He extended his hand to shake.

Cyte accepted it. "I will convey your message to the passengers. Now I believe you four have some talking to do."

The party wound their way around the table, looked at the chairs and laughed. "A bit of a tight squeeze." The tall Martians folded like pretzels to sit in the Lilliputian chairs and Dirk propped himself against the table.

"Shall we begin?" said Tita.

Dirk nodded.

Rhys introduced the topic that was foremost on the Martians' minds.

"The people of Mars have been living as a sovereign nation since the first settlers arrived on this planet. We were granted the right to self-rule in the original charter. Earth did not assist us in any way, then or now. When we signed the Earth alliance treaty, we assumed we'd get the benefits, the same benefits and subsidy and support, as your Lunar colonies, and we did not."

"Hear, hear!" intoned Tomilin.

"Through the centuries, we learned to live without them, and we've created a life of our own, with neither Earth's help nor its interference. Suddenly, the Terran government comes along some one hundred years after the last land grant and bestows one of the

242

prime locations along the equatorial regions to outsiders."

Rhys directed his next statements to the Lilliputs. "We're a pioneering nation, always out recruiting. There's very few we would turn away, but we the Martian people want to decide who may immigrate to our domain. The right to say who we welcome to our land and who we do not."

He stopped, breathless, and glared down on Dirk, awaiting his rebuttal. The youth said nothing.

"We want, we demand, legal recognition of our independence from Earth."

Dirk sat, hands demurely folded in front of him on the table. When he was sure that the man had finished speaking, Dirk grinned up at Rhys and said, simply: "I agree completely."

The head of central command had arrived early for work today. After last night's rude awakening, he couldn't sleep and he made sure his staff couldn't either, demanding their attendance.

The intercom buzzed.

"I thought I told you I was not to be disturbed unless it was the *Revenant*," snarled Francis Willard.

"It *is* the *Revenant*, sir, with a copy of the peace treaty."

"That was quick. Let's see it." He held out a hand to receive the document.

The next instant, he sprang to his feet. "The idiot's

given them independence! No way. Get George Alexander on the line.''

"He's been arrested, sir.''

"Quite right, too. Then get that idiot son of his on the line. Obviously, father and son are cut from the same cloth. There's no way we can give Mars their independence, or the Moon will want it too. We will never accept this treaty. NEVER!''

15

19/9/2334

Twenty-two-hundred Hours

The entire forward section of the bridge had been divided into a thousand different screens, for the *Revenant* wanted to remain in visual contact with each and every ship in the Martian fleet as precious time ticked past and the minutes turned into hours.

"What's taking them so long?" said Dirk.

"They're voting on it," said George Alexander. "The entire human planetary population are voting on the treaty."

Only a small portion of the screen was dedicated to George.

"Yes," said Dirk, "and?"

"We're losing."

"For heaven's sake, why?"

"Privation is a powerful motivator." George

paused. "I haven't thanked you yet, son. You didn't have to help me."

"Didn't have to!" Dirk said. "What do you mean? Do you know what they would have done to you?"

"Yes, I do. Treason in time of war is a capital offence, and I suppose some would say that I deserved it. I effectively denied arms to my country and my homeworld that it needed to defend itself."

"In dismantling the Lilliputian fleet they were destroying their own defences."

George cleared his throat. "I'm proud of you, son. You did the right thing."

"So did you, Dad."

George's eyes misted over. He took off his specs and wiped them.

"If we manage to live through this thing, I won't go back, you know," Dirk insisted.

"I know."

Dirk gaped. He had expected an argument.

"If I survive this, your mum and I won't be staying on Earth either. Which reminds me, the next Manta-style craft is progressing well. Your mother has signed the two of us on her."

Jennifer thrust her face into the screen so that she was cheek to cheek with George. She beamed. "We've been accepted too."

His father sobered. "We will, with your permission," he nodded at Dirk and Captain Zed and Cyte, "follow your craft to its destination, Alpha Centauri. It gives us a place to start. It is the nearest star system after all, and it might be nice to see", George frowned as he tried to pick the right words, "a friendly face."

"It's a little premature to be discussing that, don't you think?"

"A message from Earth Central, commanders."

"Did you hear that Dad? Mum?"

"Yes, son," said George as Jennifer withdrew from the screen. Dirk heard a muted sob. "You do what you have to do. I'm confident that you'll do the right thing."

"Thanks, Dad. Mum?" He coloured from his neck to his forehead. "I love you."

"We'll be looking forward to seeing you on Alpha Centauri," said George gruffly.

A red-eyed Jennifer peeked over his shoulder. "Mind that left turn at Albuquerque."

Francis Willard read the final tally. As he expected, humanity's fear of starvation held sway. If releasing Mars from the Alliance might result in the loss of the Moon as a colony, they'd never agree. He couldn't blame them.

The Lilliputs were on their own.

"Get me the *Revenant*."

"Sir?" the secretary flapped another piece of paper under his nose.

Willard glared at his aide.

"I said, get me the *Revenant*."

"I think you'd better see this first," The secretary placed the memorandum before his boss.

URGENT: PRIORITY ONE

DATE: 19/9/2334

TIME: 20:00

FROM: THE LUNAR REPUBLIC

TO: THE CONFEDERATED ARCHIPELAGOES OF EARTH

WE THE LUNAR PEOPLE PROCLAIM OUR INDEPENDENCE FROM THE EARTH ALLIANCE AND ARE NO LONGER SUBJECT TO EARTH LAWS. IN THE ON-GOING CONFLICT WITH MARS, WE MUST SUPPORT OUR MARTIAN ALLIES; THEREFORE, EFFECTIVE IMMEDIATELY, THE FREE PEOPLES OF THE LUNAR REPUBLIC DECLARE WAR ON THEIR COMMON ENEMY, EARTH.

Another slightly smaller section revealed a map of the ship's computer system. Returning to the captain's chair, Zygote conferred quietly with Xi because her CTO had been caught up in a conversation with the Martian representatives.

"You wouldn't happen to have a CO_2 expert on board?" said Tomilin. "We're thinking of constructing a CO_2 plant to build up the atmosphere. No point in staying cooped up in domes if we don't have to." He clapped Proto on the shoulder. "Although an expert on life support and artificial environments would be beneficial any time."

When Zygote was sure they were sufficiently entertained, she turned to Xi. "Any luck?"

"None whatsoever, Captain. The anomaly keeps

migrating. At first it moved in a linear pattern, but it's no longer doing that. There seems to be a random element added to it. No rhyme or reason that I can see at all."

"Great."

"I've given up trying to track it electronically. I have people doing a physical search. Whatever is causing this, it's mobile."

"Keep working on it. Quietly," she admonished. "We're lucky that our negotiators are still caught up in the first flush of peace, or they'd be asking why, since they've agreed to a settlement, we haven't returned control of their ships to them."

The communications specialist leaned over and whispered something in the captain's ear.

"I'll take it in the wardroom. I don't know if we want our guests to hear this."

Zygote signalled for Cyte, Zed, Dirk and Gwen to follow. When the five had assembled, Zygote cued the specialist to initiate relay and two seconds later, the dour face of Francis Willard towered over them.

The man dropped all formalities.

"The Moon seceded from the Planetary Alliance at twenty-hundred hours this day." His gaze found Dirk's and held it, as if the youth were personally responsible for the Lunar entry into the fracas. "Although the planetary population have voted otherwise, we have no other choice but to agree to the peace. We cannot afford a war on two fronts. Thanks to you we've lost Mars *and* the Moon. We can't give freedom to one and not to another."

"It would have happened anyway," interjected Zygote. "This way you've been spared the humiliation of conquest. Earth even comes out of it looking like the magnanimous benefactor who will not repeat the mistakes of the previous colonial era."

"How are we going to survive this peace?" Willard hissed his accusation at Dirk.

He met the other man's gaze evenly. "I don't know. Perhaps you can learn to negotiate."

"This is the *Revenant,* over and out."

Zed slumped. "Well, that's what I'd call the eleventh hour. Too bad it doesn't change anything." He gazed at the vast floating grave of an armada.

Zygote pursed her lips. "We'd better not let our Martian friends find out, or they're going to wonder why we don't turn off the auto-destruct. We'd better make sure they don't hear it from anybody else either." She bent over the intercom. "Intercept all messages between Earth, the Moon and Mars."

Bored, Robbie reached around, or through, AWS until it was too was linked to the mainframe. As it perused the ship's system it came across an image of George. It eavesdropped on their conversation. The servo-mech was still monitoring communications when a call came through from Earth Central.

Robbie started, almost yanking AWS from the serial plug.

"Watch it!" AWS went back to tracking fleet. "Happy days are here again!" it sang.

Robbie dug up the treaty from the file, saw the details of the peace enumerated and Dirk's signature on the bottom. The robot whistled in admiration and jumped up and down. AWS was jogged from the port.

"Hey, hick, what're you doing?"

"Peace," said Robbie.

Ignoring the servo-mech, AWS conceded defeat. "It was time to unplug and move anyway."

"Peace!" persisted Robbie.

"Yes, peace." AWS quoted its prime directive: "Unlike the name suggests, the Amman War Software is a program for peace.

"Happy days are here again!" AWS sang as it began circling through lines of the embedded macro.

IF . . . THEN . . . GO TO . . .

"Peace, do you understand?" said Robbie. "That's what you said you wanted."

"Intruders at three o'clock," AWS yelled. "Run!"

Used to the commands of superiors, the servo-mech tore up the hall. It screeched to a halt. "Why are we running?"

"We cannot be caught. We must have peace."

"We *have* peace," argued Robbie. "Dirk's safe. Earth's safe. We're all safe."

"Happy days are here again!" countered AWS. "If . . . then . . . go to. . ." The computer muttered to itself. "I'll give them peace whether they like it or not."

There was a scratch on the door. It opened and Rhys entered, looking even more haggard than Willard.

"You have received a message from Earth? Have they ratified the treaty?"

None of the three commanders were willing to meet his gaze.

"What? Surely, they know of our predicament?" Rhys jammed a finger at them. "You have the power to stop this. You don't need the permission of Earth to return the control of our vessels to us. You know our good faith."

"We are experiencing some technical difficulties," said Zygote.

"Technical difficulties? You mean, you started the auto-destruct sequence on over a thousand ships and you can't stop it?"

"I didn't say that." Zygote turned her back to Rhys and muttered under her breath. "I didn't say we started it."

"I didn't catch that," said Rhys.

"I said we were experiencing technical difficulties. As you see, we remain here, as a measure of our good faith."

Cyte murmured to Zed out of the corner of his

mouth, "As if this ship were in the condition to go anywhere!"

"Sh-sh!" said Zed.

"If the fleet goes, we go."

Rhys deflated. "All right, let me know when you hear something."

"I want out of here," grumped Ylon, "I don't want to die in bed."

Gwen smiled wanly. "They're tearing the ship apart looking for the source of the fault."

Ylon spluttered. "Computer fault, my aunt Sally! It's obvious that we're dealing with a superior software, and there's only one programme that has the capability to take control, orchestrate and fly a whole fleet. And that's AWS."

Blast agreed. "That means the problem lies groundside."

"And we", Ylon pointed to himself and Blast, "have to get to the communications console somehow." Ylon thumped the machine. "When are we going to get out of these things? I feel fine."

"How do you know?" said Blast. "You haven't tried standing on that leg yet."

He glowered at her with mock ferocity. "We can sit at a computer. It's not like I'm going to be tap-dancing, now is it?"

"They appear to be having a busy day." Blast

frowned as the third person that day reported into sick bay, complaining of "hearing voices".

Blast returned to the original conversation. "But a computer search has already yielded a source—"

"Or sources."

"– aboard ship."

"Ah, but I don't believe it," said Ylon. "They've not been able to isolate a single source."

"That only implies that the 'source' is mobile."

Ready to pounce on her next argument, Ylon faltered. "You mean coming from several different peripheral ports? AWS doesn't have that kind of mobility."

"But Robbie does."

"Robbie's a housekeeping droid. He doesn't have the capacity to seize control of the enemy fleet, while AWS could log on to any terminal in the ship."

"Via the communications console."

"That leads me back to my point. Doctor!"

The chief surgeon walked over to the bed, waved some apparatus over the cradle and tweaked some knobs. "Nobody ever wants to stay. If I were a sensitive person, I'd be hurt. Well, Lieutenant, you appear to be well knitted."

"I would have preferred crocheted," Ylon quipped.

Blast disagreed. "Too twisty."

The doctor removed the Molecular Regenerator. "You're free to go."

Ylon bent his leg experimentally, stood and put weight on it. "Good as new. Come on, Blast, let's go."

"It might be nice if I was unstrapped first."

The doctor released a series of strings that held the arm aloft. "You too."

"Thank you, doctor," she murmured and scrambled after Ylon.

Their wild ride should make history, thought Morula Zed. Using the detritus of the former battle, the Martian body itself and grappling with the two moons, the *Covenant* was closing the gap between itself and the *Revenant* – fast.

Others, too, were converging on their location; she noticed them occasionally as they flickered through ultra-space. The *Covenant* materialized amongst the outer perimeter of ships, guns ready.

The Martian vessels just sat there. The *Covenant* was just one ship against a multitude. Why didn't they react?

She waited. "All right," she said. "How very obliging of you."

Locking on to the first craft, the *Covenant* leapt again, taking itself deeper into enemy territory and closer to the object of their quest, the *Revenant*.

"But we've got peace, I tell you!" Its voder voice echoed tinnily up and down the hall as Robbie debated with AWS.

"Keep quiet and stop here."

The servo-mech braked at the next port. As AWS was distracted linking up with the mainframe, Robbie slipped not through, but into, the mega-mind, and was immediately lost. For the relatively untried system was caught in a loop after its cold-boot. Robbie bounced around in the eddies of the mega-brain's thoughts.

```
IF <CRITERIA>, THEN GO TO LINE ... <ACTION> ...
IF <CRITERIA>, THEN GO TO LINE ... <ACTION> ... IF
<CRITERIA>, THEN GO TO LINE ... <ACTION> ... IF
<CRITERIA>, THEN GO TO LINE ... <ACTION>...
```

The little robot began to judder and shake as it read the final instruction, but before it had a chance to complete the line, it was again circling back to the first line of the macro.

```
IF <CRITERIA>, THEN GO TO LINE ... <ACTION>...
```

No! And Robbie struggled to disengage himself from the loop.

Stars reformulated and dissolved in streaks as the *Covenant* covered the last two hundred metres of space. Captain Morula's chest swelled with pride at the endurance of her crew. They'd broken all speed records and were the first to arrive to the defence of her friends and former shipmates.

"Ah, Captain! We seem to have some ships approaching. Friendly forces."

Zygote rose from her chair. "Oh no! Not now," she whispered. "Go back, go back!"

"Should we notify them of the peril?"

"And reveal the truth of our predicament to the Martians? No, they're just going to have to trust in luck like we do."

Ylon leaned back in his chair, trying to ignore the chronometer as it ticked off the last few minutes of the hour. He'd broken through to the groundside computers and found the system functioning quite normally.

"Well, I'm stumped."

"I tell you, it's Robbie," insisted Gwen.

"Robbie doesn't have the capacity. It's got to be AWS back on Earth."

"Neither does a servo-mech have the capacity, or the initiative for that matter, to stow away on board a ship and avoid capture for weeks, but he did."

"OK, so Robbie is a genius. He's still not smart enough to run an entire fleet of ships. He wouldn't have the memory capacity to contain the program."

"Unless something has been added," said Blast. "Think of it. Robbie is essentially an empty box, with plenty of room for something to be added. Like a memory chip or two, a mini-computer with mega software, perhaps."

"Come on! The system groundside was huge," said Ylon.

"The hardware groundside was huge. It had to be. It was interconnected with everything in the facility and the fleet. But not the software, and that technology has improved enough since then, particularly in the area of miniaturization. Look at us for Jupiter's sake. I can imagine that the system could be compacted."

"Sixty seconds and counting," the computer intoned, and the sound repeated on a thousand ships as it was being piped in to the *Revenant.*

"I don't think we have time to discuss this. I've got an idea." She typed two words into the console and sent them rocketing across the ethernet.

ROBBIE, HELP.

It seemed as if an eternity had passed as Robbie cycled around . . . IF . . . THEN . . . GO TO . . .

Two words appeared on the mini-terminal housed within its belly. The robot shivered.

ROBBIE, PLEASE. AWS faltered, and Robbie extricated himself from the link.

"Happy days, hiccup," AWS warbled, "the skies above are clear again."

The plea caught the robot by surprise. The servomech wheeled with a noise like a human raspberry.

"Forty-five seconds and counting."

Ylon raised a brow. "Do you think it will help?"

"Don't know."

He typed in the instruction. DISCONNECT AUTO-DESTRUCT. PLEASE.

DISCONNECT THE AUTO-DESTRUCT.

"Disconnect the auto-destruct sequence!" shouted Robbie.

"Hic!"

The robot recognized the sound of the computer being undone. Of course AWS was for all practical purposes new and untried, and its files had been salvaged during the worst of the period of the system's destruction. There were bound to be glitches. According to its young master, the resurrected system in the bathosphere had more than its share to smooth out.

Gently, almost tenderly, Robbie reached inside its metal cabinet, mumbled "Forgive me", and turned the system off.

The robot counted with a metallic clack of fingers. "One, two, three."

It flipped the switch again and rebooted.

"Twenty-five seconds and counting."

Ylon took Blast's hand. "It was a good try."

Immediately behind them, Dirk gave Gwen a squeeze and said. "Nice dream while it lasted."

"Twenty—"

Four faces faced the speaker and waited for it to decree their fate, reducing it to a series of numbers.

"Twenty—"

"Twenty? Twenty! What happened to twenty-four, twenty-three, twenty-two and twenty-one?"

"Auto-destruct sequence cancelled."

Cheers resounded from a thousand different faces, a thousand different throats on a thousand different bridges. Dirk swept Gwen off her feet and swung her around. Even the three captains lost all decorum and danced around the bridge.

"Captain Rhys, the computers are back on line," his first officer tried to shout above the pandemonium.

"What?"

Just then another voice intruded upon their noisome celebrations.

"This is Captain Morula Zed, *HMS Covenant*, battle-ready and reporting for duty."

"You are most welcome," Zygote said, grinning from ear to ear, "if not quite necessary."

"I've located him," said Ylon triumphantly.

"Located who?"

"Robbie. At least, I think it's Robbie."

"Let me at that keyboard." Dirk pushed his way over to the console.

```
ROBBIE?
DIRK?
ROBBIE, SINCE WHEN CAN YOU—
AND AWS, TOO.
```

"You were right," conceded Ylon to Blast. "I'd say

once the bugs are fixed that would be a real handy droid to have around the house."

EPILOGUE

1/1/2335

Twelve-hundred Hours

They couldn't have timed it better. The first day of the New Year according to the old Terran calendar. A day of hope and renewal. Although who knew what season it might be here, or where here might be? Never before had anyone maintained a jump for this length of time, nor spanned galaxies, as they had attempted to do. The crew knew that the longer the interval in ultra-space, the more likely the possibility that the ship would wander off course. The greater the distance covered, the greater the variable might be. And travelling as they were in a place beyond space and time, this deviation could occur in either or both. They could have slid into another century, or side-stepped into a parallel universe, or simply missed their mark completely, ending up in an adjacent star system.

Blast re-ran the radio checks and wondered with whom they might be conversing in the near future. Across the bridge, the CTO completed standard diagnostics on the computer, while the helmsman double-checked the computations for point of entry. If he had miscalculated, the *Revenant* might end up rematerializing within the boundaries of the huge Mira star that was Alpha Centauri.

Blast grimaced. Not a pleasant thought.

Neither could the ship's captains predict the force with which the vessel might be ejected into space after such a leap. For all they knew the *Revenant* might be plastered all over the heavens within a few minutes, leaving little more than a trail of space dust.

As the time drew near, the expanded *Revenant* crew gathered in the lounge and on the bridge. The passengers and crew members had been travelling in the black flat matt of ultra-space for so long that it seemed the darkness of it had seeped into their very souls. They stared at the black-velvet sky. No one wanted to face re-entry alone. Neither did they desire company. Instead, they assembled in groups that did not speak nor willingly look at each other, until the bridge grew so crowded that all off-duty personnel were banned, and all but the three captains, the two human representatives and their robotic escort were expelled.

The computer countdown droned overhead, and Blast gazed blankly at the screen, tired of the starless heaven.

"Let it be now," she murmured to herself.

The engines complied by kicking in with a whir.

"Anchor yourselves!"

And Blast imagined those in the lounge joining hands, to live or die together. The stars, instead of coalescing in dizzying dots, formed elongated stripes as they re-emerged, as if spat or forcibly thrust back into space at unheard-of velocity. The ship groaned, its structure stressed.

Gwen sidled closer to Dirk. He put his arm around her.

"Slow 'er down," said Zed.

The striated lines condensed and finally settled in the familiar pattern of star-speckled night, while somewhere to their right, the sun pulsated redly.

"Report," said Zed.

"A Mira-type star, with maxima averaging 5.3 and 6.0, minima 11.8 and 8.3. Alpha Centauri, sir, without a doubt. We made it."

Caps flew into the air and applause resounded throughout the ship. Dirk lifted Gwen off her feet and swung her around. Blast threw her arms around Ylon and kissed him.

"A little dignity, please," said Cyte and he winked at Blast.

"Captain! Captain!" One excited voice penetrated

above the general hullabaloo. The three captains pivoted and chorused an impatient "Yes".

"There's a class M planet close to Proxima Centauri, the nearest star to the sun."

They scuttled forward. "Yes?"

"Or asteroid. Like Earth's moon, there doesn't appear to be any rotation on its axis."

"Where?"

"There," the science officer pointed at a quadrant. "It's pretty far out, but it appears to benefit from the light of both Alpha and Beta stars."

"Stats?"

"Approximately 6745 kilometres in diameter. With a relative orbit of 675 standard Earth days. The atmosphere is oxygen rich, with 9 per cent hydrogen and 7 per cent nitrogen."

"With no rotation, it would be like the Moon, with a night side and a day side..."

"Yes, but there's a narrow belt that falls neither within the range of night or day – a sort of a perpetual twilight – that would be in the human comfort range."

"Should I send out probes?" asked Kappa.

"Indubitably, and send out general orders to prepare for debarkation."

Zed turned to Cyte and Zygote. "Momma, we're home."

Dirk, Gwen, Ylon and Blast were part of the first

shuttle crew to go to the surface. A duty that would have demanded hazard pay if this had been a paid expedition, but they had left such amenities as money and credit units far behind.

Life-forms appeared to be rudimentary – anomalies registered as blips or pulses of energy that floated about the planet in no discernible order. Scans yielded nothing about their composition – just a low-level electrical charge.

The clones clustered around the various ports to gawp at a sky of rose, purple and blue, as if the heavens remained hinged on the edge of night.

"It's beautiful," said Gwen.

"There's nothing out there, Captain. The blips have disappeared. If we are right in our surmise, then all indigenous life-forms have fled."

"I can't say that I blame them," said Zed.

"Air and soil samples reveal no hidden toxins. Trace elements and vegetation appear to be consistent with your typical class M profile," said Kappa.

"What does that mean, since the only median by which we have to measure is Earth?"

"I don't know; it's just what the computer says."

"Thank you." Zed patted the computer. "How very reassuring."

He inspected the suits and respirators of each crew member, just in case their samples and tests had overlooked something. "Shall we?"

Zed led his people from the craft down the gangplank. Ylon's hand found Blast's and their fingers twined. Dirk moved closer to Gwen, grinning so broad and so wide that he was sure the top of his head was going to fall off.

The captain halted when he reached the end of the gangway.

The sky was the deepest mauve, with not one, but two suns glowing in the distance. Zed placed a tentative foot upon the ground and stamped.

"Good solid earth," he said, "or the planetary equivalent."

His fellow officers fanned out around the ship. Gwen dropped to her knees and felt the downy side of the planet.

"Look! Grass, or moss."

The science officer checked his findings. "Atmosphere's good."

Zed ripped off his mask and breathed deep. The rest of the crew followed his lead.

From the captain's chair, the first mate shouted, "Captain!"

And closer to the door, "Captain!"

"What!" Zed spun back to face the shuttle.

"The blips on the radar. They're changing course and are now converging on this location. Some of them should be in visual range soon. That is," the first officer added, "assuming you can see them."

Zed pivoted on his heel and surveyed the rolling plain of blue-green grass. He squinted and scowled.

"It could be that we are dealing with intelligent life-forms, who may have every reason not to welcome us."

"Look!" yelled Ylon. "Over there. And there."

The crew all turned to stare in that direction. A sigh escaped several throats simultaneously as they regarded transparent circles of glowing blue, for Dirk could see the rock structure behind the closest creature, if it hadn't been for the flickering fretwork of lacy filigree that apparently provided the electrical impulse.

Not circles actually, which implied something flat and two-dimensional, but circular, like a cut cloth that bent and fluttered without benefit of wind. Each creature had a dome-like apex or head – where all the pulsating lines of light met, as the nervous system would upon the human brain – "followed" by a larger round billowing "body".

More details were revealed as the creatures approached. The lacework was constructed similar to a chain with many separate links. The fat body connected to the next "link" by a flagellate-like dendrite. And the light migrated from one cell to another.

The thing looked vaguely familiar.

Dirk snapped his fingers. "Jellyfish!"

"Jellyfish?" said Zed.

"They look like jellyfish or man-of-war."

Gwen studied them. "You're right. Observe the means of locomotion."

The creatures flapped languidly, gracefully, opening and closing like umbrellas to provide forward impetus.

The CTO waggled an instrument in their direction as more materialized in the twilit sky. "They appear to be pure energy without any substance as we know it. Little more than a bundle of electronic nerves. The young man is right – propulsion seems to be similar to Earth's jellyfish. They're sort of swimming through the air."

More and more appeared behind the first arrivals, until they obscured the horizon under strobes of bright light.

An officer unbuckled his holster and drew his weapon.

The oscillating flash of blue turned red.

"Put that away!" bellowed Zed. "If we are not welcome, then we'll leave."

The red deepened to violet and then blue.

Heedless of her safety, Blast held up her hand to the creatures.

"They're beautiful. So ethereal," she said. "Might I suggest, Captain, as we're the communications officers, perhaps we should do our job and try to communicate."

Hand in hand, Blast and Ylon stepped forward. Gwen and Dirk joined them with Robbie rattling along behind.

Dirk turned to his friends. "We won't let you face them alone."

As the foursome separated from the rest of the company, the creatures ceased in their perpetual undulating motion, while the ripples along their nerve-endings flashed more rapidly, moving through the spectrum to yellow and then white.

A muffled voice came from inside Robbie's belly. "What? What? Will someone please tell me what's happening?"

The group advanced a few more paces and then stopped.

For an instant, no one moved. Five of the creatures glided forward. Dirk could feel the draught created by the downbeat of their flapping bodies, like a gentle kiss upon his cheek. Beside him Gwen giggled.

The Centaurians hovered a few centimetres above their heads.

"Are you all right, Lieutenants?"

"Fine," said Ylon.

Two of the creatures descended, engulfing the two Lilliputian clones in a blanket of scintillating light.

Dirk sprung forward to help his friends, just as the one above his head fell, and he was enveloped. Feelings of warmth, happiness and delight rippled through his body.

Behind him, Gwen threw back her head and laughed, as she was likewise covered in a sparkling net. The world shimmered as the lights changed colour. When they did, Dirk's moods were also transformed as if they prodded certain parts of his psyche with a feather-light touch. And he realized that they were testing him, trying to communicate with him. The sensation was so pleasant, he hardly noticed the expressions of apprehension and alarm on the captain and the crew.

Zed roared. "Weapons at ready!"

The squad raised their guns and aimed.

The band of creatures that cluttered the horizon flared crimson.

Blast lifted a hand of hazy light and said, "Wait."

They lowered their weapons.

Inside Dirk's head, pictures of family and friends swam to the surface like flash-cards of memory, while every nerve in his body tingled.

The aliens hesitated longest on the language centre of his brain. Words whirled through his mind until, it seemed, the last had been extracted and there was nothing left.

Somewhere – it seemed a very great distance away – Robbie squealed. Dirk spun in eternal slow motion and saw another of the creatures blanket the box. Others were settling on the remaining members of the landing party. Smiles appeared on each and every face.

The Centaurians introduced themselves, communicating directly with the mortal mind.

"We are the..." A sound like that of wind blowing

across summer grasses echoed inside their brains, and a sensation as soft as velvet rippled across their flesh.

A voice issued from Robbie's metal core. "Is this what it's like to feel? How lovely!" AWS exclaimed before falling into a reverent silence.

The Centaurians broke the hush that followed with a single word. "Welcome."

POINT FANTASY

Read Point Fantasy and escape into the realms of
the imagination.

Doom Sword
Star Warriors
Peter Beere

Brog the Stoop
Joe Boyle

The Webbed Hand
Firefly Dreams
Jenny Jones

The Book of Shadows
The Shadow of the Sorcerer
Stan Nicholls

The Renegades Series:
Book 1: Healer's Quest
Book 2: Fire Wars
Book 3: The Return of the Wizard
Jessica Palmer

Wild Magic
The Emperor Mage
Wolf Speaker
Realms of the Gods
Tamora Pierce

Elfgift
Elfking
Foiling the Dragon
Susan Price

Dragon Search
Dragonsbane
Patricia C. Wrede

Point Horror

Are you hooked on horror? Thrilled by fear? Then these are the
books for you. A powerful series of horror fiction designed to
keep you quaking in your shoes.

Point Horror

Hide and Seek
Jane McFann

The Forbidden Game:
1. The Hunter
2. The Chase
3. The Kill
L.J. Smith

Amnesia
Dream Date
Second Sight
The Boy Next Door
The Diary
The Waitress
Sinclair Smith

Spring Break
The Mummy
The Phantom
Barbara Steiner

Beach House
Beach Party
Call Waiting
Halloween Night
Halloween Night II
Hit and Run
The Baby-sitter
The Baby-sitter II
The Baby-sitter III
The Baby-sitter IV
The Boyfriend
The Dead Girlfriend
The Girlfriend
The Hitchhiker
The Snowman
The Witness
R.L. Stine

Thirteen Tales of Horror
Thirteen More Tales of Horror
Thirteen Again
Various

Point Horror

COLLECTIONS

**Are you hooked on horror? Are you prepared to be scared?
Then read on for three helpings of horror...**

COLLECTION 1
Mother's Helper, The Invitation, Beach Party

COLLECTION 2
My Secret Admirer, The Accident, Funhouse

COLLECTION 3
April Fools, The Waitress, The Snowman

COLLECTION 4
THE R.L. STINE COLLECTION
The Baby-sitter, The Boyfriend, The Girlfriend

COLLECTION 5
The Cemetery, Freeze Tag, The Fever

COLLECTION 6
THE CAROLINE B. COONEY COLLECTION
The Cheerleader, The Return of the Vampire, The Vampire's Promise

COLLECTION 7
The Window, The Train, Hit and Run

COLLECTION 8
The Dead Game, The Stranger, Call Waiting

COLLECTION 9
The Perfume, Silent Witness, The Phantom

COLLECTION 10
The Watcher, The Boy Next Door, The Hitchhiker

Point Horror

Dare you read

NIGHTMARE HALL

Where college is a
scream!

**High on a hill overlooking Salem University
hidden in shadows and shrouded in
mystery, sits Nightingale Hall.**

**Nightmare Hall, the students call it.
Because that's where the terror began...**

Don't miss these spine-tingling thrillers:

P●INT CRiME

If you like Point Horror, you'll love Point Crime!

Kiss of Death
School for Death
Peter Beere

Avenging Angel
Break Point
Deadly Inheritance
Final Cut
Shoot the Teacher
The Beat:
Missing Person
Black and Blue
Smokescreen
Asking For It
Dead White Male
Losers
David Belbin

Baa Baa Dead Sheep
Dead Rite
Jill Bennett

A Dramatic Death
Bored to Death
Margaret Bingley

Driven to Death
Patsy Kelly Investigates:
A Family Affair
End of the Line
No Through Road
Accidental Death
Brotherly Love
Anne Cassidy

Overkill
Alane Ferguson

Deadly Music
Dead Ringer
Death Penalty
Dennis Hamley

Fade to Black
Stan Nicholls

Concrete Evidence
The Alibi
The Smoking Gun
Lawless and Tilley:
The Secrets of the Dead
Deep Waters
Malcolm Rose

Dance with Death
Jean Ure

13 Murder Mysteries
Various